THE
UNLOVED

From the Diary of Perla S.

Books by Arnošt Lustig

THE UNLOVED

DITA SAXOVA

DARKNESS CASTS NO SHADOW

A PRAYER FOR KATERINA HOROVITZOVA

DIAMONDS OF THE NIGHT

NIGHT AND HOPE

In Czech

NEMILOVANÁ (Z DENÍKU SEDMNÁCTILETÉ PERLY SCH.)

MILÁČEK

HOŘKÁ VŮNĚ MANDLÍ

BÍLÉ BŘÍZY NA PODZIM

NIKOHO NEPONÍŽÍŠ

MODLITBA PRO KATEŘINU HOROVITZOVOU

MŮJ ZNÁMÝ VILI FELD

DITA SAXOVÁ

ULICE ZTRACENÝCH BRATŘÍ

TMA NEMÁ STÍN

DÉMANTY NOCI

NOC A NADĚJE

THE UNLOVED

From the Diary of Perla S.

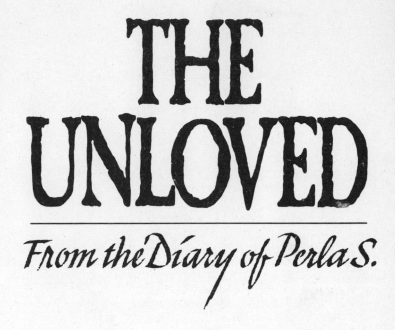

— A NOVEL BY —

ARNOŠT LUSTIG

MACMILLAN

ISBN 0-333-42239-2

First published in Great Britain 1986 by
MACMILLAN LONDON LIMITED
4 Little Essex Street London WC2R 3LF
and Basingstoke

Associated companies in Auckland, Delhi, Dublin,
Gaborone, Hamburg, Harare, Hong Kong,
Johannesburg, Kuala Lumpur, Lagos, Manzini,
Melbourne, Mexico City, Nairobi, New York, Singapore
and Tokyo.

Published in the United States of America 1985
by Arbor House Publishing Company and in Canada by
Fitzhenry & Whiteside Ltd.

Printed by The Garden City Press Ltd, Letchworth, Herts.

PART I

August 1, 1943. Once. A barrette and a comb.

August 6. Three times. A walking stick. A lady's umbrella. A fountain pen and a vial of blue ink.

August 11. Six times. A glass of baby formula made from thinned milk. A knapsack and men's galoshes. A lady's overnight bag made of vulcanized fiber. An eighth of a loaf of rye bread. Some supplementary coupons for hard workers.

It is now the eleventh day that I've been sleeping in the attic next to the Fire House on L Street. Mr. L. had a garret fixed up for me. From the skylight I can see the

3

mountains and the Hamburg Barracks, from which transports leave and at which new ones arrive. Birches and lime trees grow along the north bastion. The leaves have begun to turn yellow. First they turn yellow, then they fall off.

This morning I woke up at three o'clock. A rat who made her home here long before me scratched under the floor like a cat or a dog. I looked out through the skylight. The sky was clear, filled with August stars. I saw all of the constellations whose names I had either long ago forgotten or never known at all. It rained yesterday. But it was different than two weeks ago, when I still lived with Ludmila in the Home for Children at L 410 and we heard raindrops pounding on the pavement, on windows, trees, and drainpipes. I know it doesn't leak in here.

Once. A box of matches.

Old man O. sat up at my place almost till dawn. He talked about his travels around the world, never so much as touching me. It's enough for him just to be with me or for me to listen to him. It's not a cheap trick. I feel that he really doesn't want anything, or rather, doesn't want what for me has by now become interconnected with almost everything.

But I would bet he stares at me even when it's pitch black and he can't see as far as the tip of his nose. He's a bit odd, like a lot of people, even if they don't have a bed reserved for them in the local insane asylum. O. talked about Africa. He's got mutilated fingers; they were scorched off at the Little Fortress because he had painted what he had seen, what his interrogation officer called Greul Geschichten, horror stories.

O. gave me his impressions of the Sahara. How the sand swells like a golden sea. How one breathes as though drinking in the hot air. At the beginning of the desert there is, he says, a whole city underground, where the local people have their dwellings, horses, domestic animals, and wells, so that they live there as though living in some almost palpable night. Then he described one of their celebrations in which the natives swallow daggers or swords in the glow of tall bonfires in the middle of the night, so that the blade goes in one end of the throat and comes out the other, without a drop of blood on it. But in the daytime he never saw so much as a trace of any subterranean city; he could enter it only at night.

In the morning he took my hand, looked at me, and began to cry.

Once. A light blue Meissen salt shaker.

From where I am, it is not far to the Magdeburg Barracks that house the kitchen where I get my rations these days. Mr. L. brought me the menu of the week, *"Speisefolge der Woche."* It's good reading.

Fortunately, it is also not far to the insane asylum in the Chevalier Barracks, where the daughter of the founder of Zionism, Mr. Theodor Herzl, is locked up at the moment. Mr. L. said that geniuses mostly have dumb children and that exceptions only prove the rule. In addition, Mr. L. brought along the latest issue of their *News of the Jewish Government Council in Theresienstadt.* It informed me in German about which transports are to receive mail, when my laundry is to be delivered, and about how the administration announced a competition,

with German approval, to find names for Bastion III, the
Sheep Pen, and two or three streets. The first prize is a
can of sardines, the second a pound of flour, half a pound
of sugar, and four ounces of Sana margarine. I took no
interest in the third prize because Mr. L., as usual,
attached the verdicts of our Jewish court, to let me know
that they have a good firm hold on things. For stealing
of packages, the Jewish judges and the Jewish police
locked up eight people in the cells of Magdeburg Barracks for four weeks; one Mr. Schilling and Mr. Scheidl
were given fourteen days for not reporting to work; one
Kurt Besser got a week because his workers had run
away. Piano recitals by Sommer-Herz will take place in
the café, Hauptstrasse No. 2, Chopin on Friday and
Beethoven on Saturday. They start at 7:14 P.M. and
admission is free. The bank is open on Monday from
7:30 A.M. to 12:30 P.M., and the Central Baths on Park-
strasse, on Tuesday, Thursday, and Sunday for odd-
numbered transports. Fuel is to be conserved, of course.
I count on getting cold food and on putting up with cold
water at the baths.

Through the trees, the insane asylum built out of red
brick looks like a bakery. Farther away is the Delousing
Station, with a tall chimney and still farther along, the
post office. At one time the cavalry regiments of Empress
Maria Theresa rode through the large barracks yard of
the insane asylum. Juicy stories are told about Maria
Theresa, how she took her pick of the soldiers and, when
not enough soldiers or officers could be found, was in-
clined to choose horses.

Nothing remains of the horses. Just the stifled soil in
all the barracks yards, and on the roofs of residential
buildings and former stables where the sick lie now,
everything is grown over with green-gray moss.

It has become our custom to take a walk when

Ludmila comes by. Sometimes Milena joins us. Once, Milena said, "In any case, there is nothing worse that can happen to us."

To this Ludmila replied, "What do you mean? You could go mad."

I was more interested in just how long you can walk around, eat and sleep with it, without anyone being bothered. And I wondered whether this wasn't by some chance the case with me.

The insane take regular walks. For some of them it's something to look forward to; others probably couldn't care less. But in the yard they watch the windows barred from the outside; there must be a difference seeing the bars from the outside instead of from the inside. The shrubs all around have grown thick in two years.

I always try to guess which one is the daughter of the author of the book *The Jewish State*. But it could be any one of the women. I never could figure it out, and no one has ever confirmed it to me one way or another.

August 28. Three times. Two phonograph records. An eighth of a loaf of rye bread. Dostoevsky's *Crime and Punishment*. A travel manicure set. Twice during the night. A hot-water bottle. Four ounces of powdered sugar.

August 29. Twice. A sheaf of pink stationery. A nail file.

August 30. Five times. A collection of postcards from the most beautiful European cities and spas. An eighth of a loaf of rye bread. Two potatoes. Fifty marks in ten-mark notes. A leather frame for photographs. Once. A hand-knit woolen ski sweater.

According to Mr. L. there are three kinds of people in the world. Referees, like those at a soccer game, who put on strict and impartial faces and want everybody to accept, without argument, all their decisions, even the worst of them, as being the only right ones. Columbuses, who discover what already exists, so that instead of India for which they set out, they find America, which has been there all along. The third are Napoleons. They lead France into wars to save her, and the result is the defeat of France.

For Mr. L. the destinies of countries merely reflect human destinies, or the other way around. He thinks things have been going downhill for mankind for a good number of centuries, but unfortunately or fortunately, not for everybody at the same time; therefore, no one ever really resists. He doubts that it can be turned around. He talks about decadence, but he has never explained the exact meaning of that word to me.

Once he took me to the local catacombs and declared that this was the place where people who survive this war would live; therefore, we had nothing to envy them for.

We held hands for a while. Mr. L. called my attention to the fact that it was better not to talk in the catacombs as we could not be sure how far sound carried or who could hear it. I let his hand go. I felt that he was a step away from me. I turned to the side. Suddenly, he wasn't there anymore. I whispered. It carried far. I took a step

blindly. Somewhere far away my whisper was still fading. I did not repeat it. The air became heavy. The
darkness grew dense. The sound, the silence, boomed.
I had a knot in my throat. I felt terrible. I was afraid.
I was forcing myself to laugh. It didn't occur to me that
it was even a little funny. Where was the exit? I felt as
if I were at the end of the world, at the end of time. All
at once, I became sweaty from head to toe. Suddenly, I
felt Mr. L.'s breath, mouth, and palm against the back
of my neck. I took his hand, frightened and relieved.

Outside, I relished the light. I heard Mr. L.'s voice.
The ghetto seemed like a home to me. I think that at that
moment I hated him for needing him so much.

"No one will ever get me underground," I said. I was
looking into the sun and it almost blinded me. It was one
of the few occasions when he allowed himself to be seen
with me on the outside. "I know how those who are
blind, deaf and dumb, lost, and drowned somewhere on
the ocean floor must feel." I was thinking about people
who get lost and no longer find an exit, about people who
will no longer be helped by having been more decent
than was expected of them under circumstances when
only a few are decent. It's terrible to depend on someone
entirely, to want something I don't have, what I can only
get from others. I didn't know that in darkness everything I don't like about myself—cowardice, fear, fury—
was growing within me.

"It hasn't been this nice for a long time," I said.

He looked at me the way adults look at children. He
said I was pretty, but I wished to be crude. I don't like
mazes. I was almost angry with him for having been so
civilized all the time—the opposite of me, Ludmila,
Milena, and my acquaintances. I wished to control myself like Mr. L., to behave as if the greatest possible

failure, fear, and defeat did not touch me.

Then he must have tried to explain the meaning of the word "decadence" to me but I wasn't sure. It is "decadent" or "smart" when countries or people treat principles like toilet tissue, don't take promises to heart, whether giving or receiving them, and join or betray someone according to how or when it suits them. They cannot be trusted, and in the end they don't even trust themselves. They stab a person in the back as they embrace him. And it is hard to believe that they could possibly change for the better. They can only be stronger or weaker. In reality, they are capable of robbing and destroying the entire world just to become a penny richer. But at the same time, they say just that about their competitors and opponents; they challenge only the weak and play up to the strong.

He is obsessed with these things, as if we weren't where we are and as if he weren't just explaining it to me but rather could change the state of affairs by accurately depicting the circumstances.

He says, "Some people are not referees, Columbuses, or Napoleons. They are colorless, formless, nothing, nothing, just sheer existence. Their sole purpose is to rub shoulders with those who are better than they, who have accomplished more." I know what he meant. He knew one of our people who had never grown to army height, so he made up for it by shouting rather than talking, and at times he literally yelled just to call attention to himself.

I switched to the difference between a man and a woman. He smiled. "A women likes to talk twenty minutes before and a man not till twenty minutes after."

And he added that a woman and a man are only rarely in the same mood.

* * *

We are all getting more superstitious. Ludmila began to frighten herself with the number thirteen, in addition to black cats, which are supposed to bring bad luck when they cross your path.

Yesterday Ludmila asked, "Is it always true that each time you go to bed with someone you risk gaining a body and losing the friendship that led you to it? Do you ever get more than you expect and do you ever give more than you are expected to?"

I replied, "Lidushka, some people steal and others lie. For some, life is like a bank robbery: On the one hand, you take a risk, and on the other, if you can do it without much thought, you can take whatever you happen to find in the safe."

At that, Ludmila remained silent.

Then I looked out and pointed to the church tower, which was striking five o'clock. "There are things that repeat themselves, and things that happen only once. And there are people for whom things repeat themselves and people for whom things happen only once. For ten days I've been listening to those beautiful, slow bells that are like the heart of something grand, so grand that I don't understand it, but I know that it's not for me.

"I don't even know how many hundreds of years the tower has been standing here or how many hundreds of years old the bell is in the belfry, but I can imagine that in all those centuries the bells have tolled just as they do now, slowly, thoroughly, without changing their voice or rhythm, and that they will keep on tolling that way for many hundreds of years to come, unless there is an earthquake or a flood. And unlike you or me, they won't promise anything but spring, summer, fall, and winter, birth, death, or anniversary, while you and I don't even

know what tomorrow will bring or what is still ahead this
evening or during the night."

Five times. A candle. A jar of strawberry jam. Winter
socks. Twenty-five marks. Eleven marks.

Once. Five yards of electric wire with a plug at each
end. A box of safety pins.

Milena had an acquaintance in the columbarium
where they collect the ashes of the people who have died,
before pouring them into the Eger for the good of the
fish .in the sea. According to Mr. L., it's up to three
hundred people a day now. And so I look at Milena and
Ludmila and at my neighbors and people I don't know,
imagining them as fish. I never imagine people as ash.
The dead are taken down in the morning in funeral
carts, hauled by people, eight in the front, eight on the
sides, and four in the back. Before and after, the carts
are used by the bakeries for the delivery of bread or for
transporting construction material.
I told Milena, "Would you believe that I still haven't
seen a dead man close up?"
I wanted her to tell me what it is she's after when she
goes to the columbarium, looking to talk to someone.
"You should get used to it," she said avoiding a direct
response.
"Perhaps I avoid the dead for the same reason you
want to get close to them."
Milena walks in high-heeled shoes, stumbles behind
the funeral cart, and looks elegant and ridiculous.
"I hope the cold will discourage you, even if the sun
didn't," I said.

* * *

In the evening I told this to Ludmila. Ludmila looked off into the distance, as if I could guess what was coming. I was almost glad when it did.

Ludmila told me, "Would you have the stomach to get involved with someone from the Casino or from the Commandant's Headquarters—you keep on looking over there?" I don't know whether she waited for me to reply.

September 1, 1943. I asked him cautiously whether he wouldn't prefer to be sitting behind an engine and flying rather than be concerned with prison technology. He just smiled. He told me, as if their German stuff made any sense to me, that their "National Socialist Revolution" demanded loyalty and boundless dedication from him in every sector, on the front as well as at home. I didn't dare ask why his loyalty didn't include his Brünnhilde.

He tried to convince me that he was different from all the others. Definitely more courageous and not as narrow-minded, to quote him exactly.

He told me I was good-looking, that my legs were out of an Albrecht Dürer painting, and that it's almost too bad I'm a Jew.

Then he told me about what he had seen and learned in other camps, of which we have not even the remotest idea and which, except for a close circle of staff officers who are in on such things, no one talks about, not even at the highest levels of German society. As far as his life here is concerned, he mentioned that he picks as collaborators those of us who don't exactly have the clearest of consciences. He protested against the use of the con-

cepts of treason and loyalty in our present circumstances. And he added that he also picks the best of us,
because in the course of things, when they have to make
a choice between worse and worst, nobody appears in the
best of lights anymore. He was surprised at how neat I
kept things here, relatively speaking that is, he added.

"A big mouse lives here with me," I said. "An old
rat."

"There really are a lot of rats here. The whole country
is full of rats, all the buildings, hallways, lofts, kitchens,
and bedrooms."

"No one exterminates them," I said.

"We've got our hands full with our work," he said
with a sigh.

When I asked him whether he wasn't afraid to come
and see me, he smiled, saying that he could kill me at
any time of the day or night, in whatever manner he
might desire, though he wouldn't need to do it himself,
and wouldn't really want to see the sight of blood.

He expected that it would make me laugh. But instead, I was thinking how the best of our people would
find themselves in the same boat as the worst ones,
rowing hand over hand to an unknown destination, one
two, one two, pretending that as soon as one survived,
everything in his past would be automatically erased.

"Where is that old rat?" he asked. I pointed toward
the corner. He fired a shot. Then he offered to make
some inquiries about my chances of getting into one of
those new institutes where they retrain women to fit the
requirements of the Nordic race.

"Don't shoot anymore," I pleaded. "People won't
understand what's going on."

I wasn't listening until he said that it was not always
necessary to shoot an entire village, an entire street, to

shoot an entire house, that it sometimes was enough to kill one person in just one house, one village, or a town and the entire building, street, and town—at times the entire country—would swear obedience to the German authorities.

There are many ways to please a man. If there was something I didn't know, I have done my best to learn it. Along the way, I tell myself how lucky I am, that many people are much worse off. I've learned not to complain or feel sorry for myself; I don't even like it when others feel sorry for me. I think I'm really relatively happy. Once, while standing on the soup line, somebody told me that I should pray because I looked sad. I thought, why not? But I don't know how to pray. I had to make up my own prayer. I don't know who decides whether a person will be happy or unhappy.

Unlike Ludmila, I don't set limits for myself. Something tells me what is acceptable and why and what isn't acceptable and why not. And what is better or worse for me, best or worst. What is best for a man is usually good for me too. In this respect I was probably born under a lucky star.

The Cabalist was once showing off his brilliance: "Men who become too preoccupied with women do so at their own risk; they become the children of hell." I imagine myself as a daughter of hell. No one has ever been there. Who knows what it's like? Over the long span of time, all ancient wisdom seems weak when you're trying to make it seem like the latest thing. He can take his whole Cabala and stuff it. But he hangs onto it as if he were drowning. Maybe he is drowning, only he doesn't know it yet. It has occurred to me several times that women don't rape men; it's the other way around. The body is a tool in a game that at times stops being amusing. But it's also the same the other way around; it is amusing, at least for me. It would be worse if it weren't. And besides, everything becomes tiresome after a while. The most astonishing things may suddenly turn into everyday affairs and just as unexpectedly become extremely interesting again with somebody else. And I ought to be glad that though I can't change my body, I can change somebody else.

According to Mr. L., we live between two floods anyway. I told Lida that in any case, it never arrives like lightning out of the clear blue sky. In addition, some guys are smart or experienced enough to know that they ought to be the first ones to tell you that it's no perversion as far as they are concerned.

I asked Lida, "Do you like lukewarm milk?"

September 2, 1943. Mr. L., a member of the Council of Elders, told me that he didn't want to talk about Theresienstadt. He proposed Monte Carlo as the topic for this afternoon's conversation, where he had once bet and lost two weeks' hotel accommodations and as a result had to return home a week before he and his wife had originally planned, or we could talk about any harbor of my choosing, as long as it wasn't Hamburg or Bremerhaven.

Mr. L. would never talk about rats, even if he saw one right at his feet.

He didn't visit me for a long time. Once, as an apology for his long absence, he quoted some French author, to the effect that love grows when undernourished, dies when overfed—just the opposite of us.

He wanted the same thing from me as the Luftwaffe officer, whom he knows nothing about, or maybe I only think he knows nothing about him, even though I intend to be as quiet as a mouse. I once told Ludmila that it's like mucus in the chest when you have a cold, and it even looks like that, though it's on me from the outside; and Ludmila looked as if she were about to be sick. I didn't say that she could keep a handkerchief at hand. Or use a piece of a man's shirt.

Mr. L. told me that we have a past but no future. It reminds him of watching a show but facing backward and of acting in it at the same time.

I stopped by at L 218. As soon as I entered the hallway, I ran into the Cabalist. A boy from his work squad, Ernie H., was standing with a shovel in his hand by a garbage pit where he had been cleaning, watching a swallow with a worm in its beak returning to its nest in a drainpipe under the roof. The swallow flew in an elegant arc and Ernie H. uttered two words, as if in a dream. The Cabalist asked in amazement, "You know something about Maxim Gorky?"

"Haven't you heard about the biggest plane in the world? Four engines on each wing? How it took off and crashed, because an escort pursuit-plane collided with it?"

The Cabalist was put at ease. He was relieved that the boy with the shovel was not as well read as he had originally feared. Ernie H. is one of those filchers who specialize in the overnight bags of freshly arrived transports, though they have never caught him doing anything that would have allowed them to make him join his friends in the Home for Wayward Children, which he visits day and night, whenever he has a free moment.

Among all the thieves, Ernie H. has always had the best reputation, because he was the first to have climbed over Bastion III into Oberscharführer Heindl's garden, from which he brought a rose to Kate Cirer so that he would be allowed to take off her panties. If, as Mr. L. used to say, there are people, even here, who have respect for the rules, Ernie H. might serve as an example of someone who has nothing but disrespect for all rules.

Once, he invited me to be his companion on an outing to L 417, the School of the First Home, the so-called Ivan Dostoevsky School, after Lichtsperre, lights out, so that I could see that even the smartest kids, the ones who publish their own journal, have not so much as a tenth of the experience he has.

On the way to L 417 he showed me a traveling alarm clock that he had filched just to show them when he returned it the next day that they weren't nearly as observant as they pretended to be.

I told Ludmila about the time I was sitting in school, dressed in a white blouse with short puffed sleeves made out of a flowery washable material, and my desk partner all of a sudden blurted out what beautiful delicate skin I had.

I turned my head to her and asked whether that was good or bad.

"Look," she said, "you have just a tiny bit of fuzz, like a peach when you hold it in your hand."

"Who cares?" I said, lying, then.

But I was thinking all the while how boys would stroke me and whether they would like it. I wasn't all that mature—my face and my skin were covered with acne. I also didn't look all that adult, breastwise.

*   *   *

Mr. L. stuck to his topic. He claimed that the greatest harbors in the world would lose their glitter, maybe even before we could get out of here, and the beautiful ships, which we discussed like paintings, musical compositions, or other works of art, would serve merely as amusement spots, restaurants, or luxury nightclubs.

Then he smiled, but one could read in his smile that our chances were one in five million.

"Will you dance with me?" I asked.

"Right now?" Mr. L. caught on. "Which ship would you like to go to? The *Normandie*? The *Queen Mary*? Both have garnered a blue ribbon for a record sailing across the ocean."

"I hope I won't get seasick."

"The rocking is not all that bad in the harbor," said Mr. L.

November 5. Once. A carry-on hatbox. Twice in the afternoon. A set of ladies winter underwear. Three times in the evening. A pair of spats. Knee socks. Nail clippers.

When it rains like this, I feel as if I were in a bottle with the water level around me rising right up to my throat.

November 6, 1943. "We are like animals," said Ludmila. "We eat like horses, standing or on the run, sleep in stables like cows, are frightened even though nothing seems to threaten us at the moment, and mostly obey like slaves. We are not even remotely as beautiful as we think we are. One out of two could be a sheep, born with four legs and with wool to shear. It makes no difference that not one out of ten or even a hundred people like it this way."

"All that is as distant from me as Monte Carlo," I said. If you want, I can tell you all about this old rat that disturbs my dreams, scratching away at the floorboards.

"Could you kill someone just because he was a German?" But she must not have cared about my answer, because she added quickly, "Why do we let ourselves be crushed, bent in half, and squeezed, without killing them back?"

"No one has killed you yet," I said, glancing her way. Lida is good-looking, almost grown up, even though adulthood to her consists of having the biggest breasts one could possibly have. She has black eyes, like a gypsy, but light, golden hair and a very dignified walk. Whenever I manage to hear her without listening, I feel like a trout in a stream with her. She is one of those people from whom I sense no threat or competition.

"I don't want to wait till it's too late," said Ludmila. Then she said, "I had a dream straight out of the Bible. About worms, lizards, insects, and maggots. I was standing in a courtyard surrounded by a big barbed-wire fence, and a gander was strutting on the garbage pile, pecking and picking up bugs and worms. Once in a while he would hold them up in his beak, raise his neck, and then let them drop down into his stomach. I know dreams have a meaning unique to each person. Nobody has yet managed to explain to me the point of sleeping, aside from getting rest. I don't understand why sometimes I suddenly feel as if I were an outcast, belonging nowhere, like a foreigner, repulsive even to myself."

I said to her, "I prefer to think of a stove filled with coal, hot smoke being drawn up the chimney, peeling the ice off the walls, and I don't need to sit with a coat on in the room, with a blanket over my knees, wearing gloves. I am obsessed with words. Words like 'fish' or 'trees,' like 'water,' 'air,' 'sky,' 'people,' 'rocks,' or 'chalk.' "

I gave Ludmila two potatoes, asking her not to thank me more than a hundred times. When she asked where I was going, I told her that I had an important meeting. Mr. L. had arranged for me to get out of joining a work squad. Other than for roll call, I don't go anywhere I don't want to go. I didn't tell her that Mr. L. gave me this black notebook, so that I could write down what women have always recorded as regularly or irregularly as their payments. I wrote down what I thought was important. When I was little, my mother used to say that lying is the worst of all sins, but she never mentioned whether that applied to lying to oneself or telling lies to someone because he lies a hundred or a thousand times more often than I have.

I went out for a stroll around the Fire House and along the park where the Casino is at one end, the Commandant's Headquarters at the other. I was daydreaming about meeting the Luftwaffe officer and savoring the fact that I would turn seventeen in just a few days.

Lida told me, "Do you also get the feeling sometimes that you aren't alive? As if it were some moving, breathing, spoken dream? As if you were waiting in line for soup and at the same time you weren't? People shove you, curse you, but you don't hear. You are and you aren't. It's such a strange existence, separated by only the thinnest of lines from nonexistence, but neither like a larva about to turn into a butterfly nor like a man lying down to wait till he falls asleep."

In response, I told Lida about how, once, when I was a little girl, my father slapped me because I had lost my new hat. In reality, I hadn't lost it but had thrown it down the elevator shaft in our building. It had been buried there for almost six months.

"It wasn't just pain that I felt," I said. "And it was quite a slap considering my father's anger and my tiny face. I wasn't even four. Have you ever been drunk?" I asked at last, knowing full well she couldn't have been yet. I wondered whether Lida and I would live to see the year 1944.

November 6. Once. A fork, a spoon, and a knife. Twice in the evening. A potato basket. A pad of writing paper, still intact. During the night twice more. A hard-boiled egg. A bag of dried carrots. A brush and some shampoo.

November 8, 1943. These days I frequent the Youth Home, a big green building on the corner of L 218 and D 417, just like the way people used to frequent biograph Roxy or Café Ascherman. Harychek Geduld, having noticed my black cotton gloves, was curious to know whether I had taken up *Entlausungsdienst* in the Delousing Station, out of boredom.

We were sitting upstairs on his bunk bed, playing Monopoly. Harychek Geduld manufactures the paper money out of cardboard. He adjusted the game as he saw fit. In addition to his constant arguing with the floor captain, the Cabalist, and his chasing after all sorts of documents pertaining to the French, the Russian, and who knows which other revolution, he composes verses about the sun, the bright dead stars, and other such encouraging topics. I rolled two sixes in a row. "Dispatch without delay two thousand stinking Jews to shovel the snow at Ruzyne Airport." Then I rolled two five times: "Return your money, bonds, jewels, watches and engagement rings to the bank, pick up a receipt, and wait to be called to a transport." Meanwhile, Harychek rolled three three times in a row: "Sail around the world in first class on a luxury liner and then return to your home port. Pay a thousand gold coins at each stop. In addition, pay for each passenger in the lower deck. Pay special premiums for having your citizenship revoked or for emigration. If you are over sixteen, pay for all the schooling that you have completed or for all retraining courses given by the state. In home port, pay for the voyage five times over." Then he rolled snake eyes: "All the harbors are closed to you. Sell your property to the municipal authority. Return to where you were three turns ago." A five is paid for with winter underwear, gloves, and furs, and the person who makes it through to the "Winter Aid" square or the *Kraft durch Freude*, "Strength Through Joy" square, hands over his belongings and moves over to the "Theresienstadt" square.

Harychek Geduld, one of the half-breeds who don't go east so long as they either are less than fourteen or their parents are not in internment, supplements Monopoly with additional squares and complications, such as, "Immediately pay additional rent for your apartment from which you were evicted two years ago." Or, "Immediately bring all the possessions, money, and jewelry that you have smuggled into the Ghetto to the Gestapo office."

There is little he enjoys as much as this. He is currently altering the board to include payments for transport east, he is simply not about to let us get something for nothing. Because they brought in some animals from Lidice, the shot-up mining village, he has added some color to the board with such livestock as sheep, cows, and chickens that the Germans have spared.

I asked him whether he had come up with any new verses, and he showed me something about a Jew who ran away into the forest, only to voluntarily turn himself in to the Gestapo after being informed that if he didn't do so by that evening, his mother, father, and brothers would be hanged. They were hanged as soon as he appeared, so that he could witness it before he too was hanged.

"Do you happen to know the saying that goes, 'One should not laugh when all around are crying?' By the same token, one shouldn't cry when everyone else is laughing."

I looked at him. He immediately drew another square: "A forest. The Gestapo is calling you. Go back fifty squares." He decided to add another square: "Exchange your transport card for a number that will not make the transport for another forty-eight hours. Pay the full amount in gold coins to the secretary of the Council of Elders with supplemental payments for his legal counsel, for the head of the Registration Department, and for the director of the Health Service. Roll the dice, and if you get a number lower than six, repeat the payment, adding a remittance for the firemen equal to what you paid to the director of the Health Service. Continue rolling till a six comes up. If you are out of funds, get ready for a transport." Then he exchanged the square *Drang nach osten* for *Drang nach oben*. "Expansion to the top."

After two hours, we got tired of it. We discussed *Rassenschande*—racial shame. This is something that weighs on Ludmila's mind more than anything. Her eyes are riveted on the German Casino building, out of which music comes once in a while, even though there is dancing there only in the evening. She let me know when the Luftwaffe officer was coming out.

Outside it's raining again. It reminds me of the Flood, dripping drop after drop rather than rushing in a tide. Harychek Geduld made a joke for our benefit, about how our great-grandfathers had learned to breathe under water for forty days.

"One girl who swallowed it for the first time dreamed that her hair fell out because of it," Ludmila said.

"Just like that? And what actually happened the first time?" I asked her.

"You know that for some girls it's the first thing they want from them. Not everyone is lucky enough to have it arrive gradually and be able to get used to it. To see several men wanting it, one after another, or just a single one, but not wanting it all at once."

"Do you want me to describe it as one of the absolute proofs of devotion?" I asked, because I know Ludmila and I'm aware of how she wants to suffuse even the coldest thing with some warmth and because we all know what we miss most. "Maybe it's something that allows a woman to express everything she's likely to go through, if you know what I mean, or is prepared to do."

"First she only caressed and kissed him and then she

did it because she was still a virgin and had no desire
not to be a virgin. At night she dreamed about it. She
dreamed that the boy was caressing and kissing her, on
the back of her neck, where she liked it best. Then she
was in the same camp as he was, without a mirror for
a long time, until she caught sight of herself in a window
and noticed that she had no hair."

"But it was just a dream, right?" I said.

"You bet, but she only dreamed it after she had
actually swallowed it."

"Did she have no hair because it had been shaved off,
the way everyone's is, or did it fall out because of illness?"

"That's only the first half of her dream," said Lida.
"Then they made love again. She was terribly in love
with him and wanted to please him in every way and also
to please herself. But at the same time, the girl could see
that the boy was losing his hair, eyebrows, and
eyelashes. The longer they made love, the thinner all of
it got, but it didn't stop there; all at once, he began to
dissolve before her eyes, and she too was dissolving,
until they both disappeared altogether. Vanished."

"How do you explain it? What could be the meaning
of such a dream?"

"You don't know?"

"I have no idea. How can I possibly know? Besides,
I don't even know whether I want to know."

"As they dissolved, like a shining star about to die but
before it dies completely and leaves a black void in the
sky, the girl had begun to cry."

"Didn't that dream of hers have three parts to it?"

"It was so beautiful that she couldn't hold it in and
she burst out crying. But at the same time it was just
awful. Dissolving, she wanted to hold onto his body, as
if she could stop it. But she didn't stop it, they kept

dissolving, ceaselessly, and as they were vanishing, they turned into an illumination, into two big circles, a red and a yellow. And these circles of light moved into each other, sucking each other in, like two flat suns seen from up close, if you know what I mean; they bumped into each other noiselessly but at the same time loudly, like when two railroad car bumpers collide into each other at a railway station, though you can't hear it, but only see it, because you're too far away. Nothing could rescue them. They just vanished. Only the dead light remained. And then the light too went out, like a dying star, leaving an empty sky."

"Is there more to the dream?" I asked.

"No, that's all," answered Ludmila. "Can you take it?"

"Thanks. If you think dreams should be shared, then fine."

To me, Ludmila seemed like that woman in Prague who knew so many languages that in the end she couldn't communicate with anyone. But I seemed that way to myself, too. Ludmila looked as if she were on the verge of tears.

"I want to get rid of it," she said.

"What happened when the girl woke up?" I asked.

"She brought him a red rose. The nicest one she could find in the garden."

"Was that a dream too? Did she do it before or after what you said she had done for the first time?"

"That was true. All was a dream," said Ludmila.

"But she didn't have to swallow it," I said quietly. "You don't have to swallow it. That girl could have held it in her mouth and given it back to him when she kissed him. Not to mention how easy it is just to spit it out." I smiled.

Lida doubled over, as if feeling sick to her stomach.

At first I thought she had just inhaled rather loudly. She burst out crying.

The following day, she and I took a stroll. She was wearing a blouse with a man's collar and a tie, like a German woman. I told Lida that people had seen Ernie H. carrying a rose over to me, after he couldn't pass up the chance to unwrap it inside the building. Lida said that I'm lucky and that things always turn out to my advantage; that I'm like a cat that always lands safely on all fours, no matter from what height it's thrown. (Since that time I've pictured myself flying from a roof and landing on all fours.) We talked about the insane, about Africa as old man O. described it to me, and about imagination. We walked by the bakery and the bread smelled so wonderful, like the smell of roses but better, because it really was the smell of baked bread; afterward we went by the foundry, where there was a smell of fire, iron, and sweat, and finally, we ended up near the insane asylum again. In the end, everything always draws us to the insane asylum.

Far away, but not so far as not to be seen, as though someone could touch them, there are mountains. For some reason, mountains give me the feeling that there is a kind of freedom that no one can shackle, not even in the worst prison, though no one has yet discovered why. It's like the joke that Mr. L. told me, about the medical students who wanted to discover the secret of life, at least with respect to rabbits and guinea pigs, so they dissected a great many animals. But they never discovered anything because the dissected animals had not one spark of life left in them. For Lida, whenever she's with me, every day is like a revelation from heaven. One day it is virginal immaculateness (ha! ha!), the next, courage (that's no longer a laughing matter), and the third, unselfishness.

I said, "What I find intriguing in my imagination is never glamorous in reality. Only a fraction of it can be carried over." But at the same time, I was thinking that it's not quite true that what is originally in the imagination cannot be carried over into reality.

The inmates were just winding up their afternoon stroll. They looked calm and desperate, some of them walking in an orderly manner and everybody, at least those I saw from up close, sad-eyed.

"As for me, when I am intrigued by an idea, I have to carry it over into reality, otherwise I might be destroyed by my imagination," Lida said, as if she'd read my thoughts. "Imagination means emptiness; reality, fulfillment."

"But it also means a beginning and an end," I said.

"Everything means a beginning and an end, each second," Lida said almost sadly. "Each breath, each fraction of a dream." I kept silent. I knew what would come.

"At times it's all upside down," Lida said. "Imagination as a dream, perversion as a lie or as the truth. But imagination, I'm telling you, is the sole reality for me sometimes. Or at least the most acceptable of realities."

Ludmila was staring at the insane, silently. She was contemplating the meaning of emptiness or fulfillment in a girl's terms, asking herself whether they are mutually exclusive, and if so, when and how. She probably also considered with whom. And how often. And also, knowing our Lida, why.

With the inmates back from their stroll, the insane asylum grew quiet. One could hear the wind; some storm clouds were surging out of the north. It looked like rain.

It was getting cool. We were walking home. Ludmila was clinging to me like my sister, my mother, or my lover. When it rains for more than an hour, the whole of Theresienstadt turns into a swamp. People who don't need to be out in the street crawl into their burrows. Streets, walls, houses—everything is full of mud, and the rain pounds down on it.

Although it has been raining persistently, I went to a soccer game that Mr. L. gave me two tickets for. It was played in the big yard of the Dresden army barracks; seven men on a side instead of eleven, because the field is narrower and shorter. This is the last game of the season, instituted by the Germans after they executed people who, in spite of the strictest rules, had sent letters to relatives describing the conditions here, or not even that much, just saying they were alive, working, and were all right.

The barracks form a large rectangle, with covered balconies on four floors. They resemble an old castle.

A group of German officers and noncommissioned officers watched from the top balcony, where they had a good view without letting themselves be seen by others. Each officer is the owner of a team, taking bets on it, both in the individual rounds and on the final outcome, giving odds, like betting at the racetrack. Sometimes they supposedly lose half their entire pay, and I hear that they've even borrowed for it.

I was looking for a blue pilot's jacket among the uniforms. Since the time the German officer visited me, I could see him only when he was coming out of the Casino or riding his horse under the bastion, and once while he was entering the hallway of the Commandant's office.

The game was Electricians against Kleidekammer. Kleidekammer won five to two. If their owner had bet a lot of money and had lost, I would bet that the defense, the goalie, and who knows who else from the midfield or the defense would very soon get a summons card for a transport east. Some officers inspect lists of transports from Prague so they can take off former players of Hagibor, or as happened once, the defense of the prewar team Polaban Nymburk, just as long as the transport from Prague is merely passing through Theresienstadt on its way farther east.

Ludmila was standing next to me, staring at the strong legs of the players, not feeling compelled to talk. We know several of the soccer players. Soccer players— unlike people who do nothing but talk about their past, hoping to retrieve it out of oblivion—remain superstars even here.

A lot of people here found out that a great many things were not nearly as important as they appeared to be. Also the importance of those people whose recognition you counted on disappeared.

Soccer, like any game, is governed by rules that apply equally to both sides, at least from the referee's opening whistle to the final one that ends the game. And the referees are like gods, each of their decisions final for at least ninety minutes. For some people soccer is the last religion.

Therefore, each match is packed, even when it rains as it did today. We like to mull over all the strategic and tactical tricks and snares connected with soccer, the same way we like to discuss who used to be what, how it has marked him, and what he is now. What people were is just as interesting as what they are now and where their fate will lead them.

We have all been tossed together, like shuffling a deck of cards or like an earthquake destroying everything. People who were never together, who only knew one another at a distance, suddenly partake in what in the old days was called a common fate. Soccer is a bridge from the past; we are privileged to watch individual players and make guesses as to what will befall them. For a number of people, soccer is worth the risk, which no one tries to hide, even though there's not much talk about it. After each serious injury, the affected player finds himself in a transport east, though a great many players would have been there long ago were it not for soccer. He hands over his uniform, sneakers and jump rope, and off he goes.

At the same time, everyone, absolutely everyone, cares that the games go on, because it is a reminder not only of what was but also of what is in each game, is best here and now, this very moment. I saw a couple of rather fierce arguments about who would play and who would sit the game out on the bench. No one ever wants to be left out because no one is sure that he will be here for the next match.

November 10. A glass of strawberry preserves. Three times. A fox fur, cut off of a man's coat. An oil lamp with a mirror and a hook, so I can hang it on a nail in the wall.

Mr. L. spent the night at my place. He talked about cormorants. Fishermen in China supposedly attach iron clamps on cormorants' necks before going out fishing, so that the birds can catch the fish without being able to swallow them.

In the morning, Ludmila asked, "You mean to tell me that you enjoy kissing him wherever he wants you to?"

And then, "Is it really like a thousand live microscopic animals flowing in a single substance, or does it taste like fish oil?"

"It's alive, just as blood is alive."

Then I laughed. "Anyone is free to taste it, if he wants to."

Then she told me what Dr. H. from Amsterdam told her. A great many people who come here from all those twenty-one countries are not quite right in every respect. As far as the relatively high number of degenerates is concerned, those with papers to certify it, that is, she was surprised to learn, it's not always to their detriment. Some of the children, for instance, may have their fingers and bones broken without feeling any pain.

One such illness manifests itself in the children who look like little birds, numbed from the cold. By the time they are three years old, it's all over for them. As they die, they supposedly feel absolutely no pain. It's an ideal, painless death, like someone falling asleep, said Lida. But that's not the only advantage. The other advantage to us of the degenerate members is that the weakest and the most mentally frail are weeded out so that we not only look stronger but as a whole are stronger. I don't find this a particularly big boost, since people may become blind or lame simply because someone in their family was and, without knowing any better, married into another similar family.

* * *

Mr. L.'s wife and children, a girl and a boy, had gone east without his being able to switch their registration cards in Central Registry. He has access there and switches cards for me when transports are being put together and sent off, though I don't know how much longer he'll be able to do it or how much longer he'll enjoy doing it.

It goes without saying that should the people from the Council of Elders find out about it, he will be gone with the first transport, as punishment. All the same, he knows that everyone with a key to the Registry, two hands, good nerves, and a strong stomach, does it. Mr. L. says that danger is beautiful, like sin.

Mostly, it's enough for him to pull my card out for the decisive twenty-four or thirty-six hours when new transports are put together and called up, occasionally also for an additional twelve to twenty-four hours until they depart. He tends to be like me in that he doesn't like it when I thank him for saving my life, because it's always at the expense of someone else's. It's like a loan that we'll never be able to pay back. Even though, fortunately, we don't know the people on the substitute cards. I, because I've never seen them and probably never will, and Mr. L., because, to be on the safe side, he'd rather not look. It's like Russian roulette, which he once spoke about. We've been lucky so far in that it hasn't misfired and we haven't recognized any names, not even afterward, with respect to the bereaved. But when Mr. L. was unable to do anything, as in the case of his family, he had to let them go.

I saw him that day and the following day as well, when he looked as though nothing had happened, like a man going out into the street unprepared for the freezing weather and wind. He was grim and said nothing, but it was like a man who says nothing because his face and lips are numb from the cold; so even if he did try to talk, it would come out distorted, like frozen people who try to speak.

When Mr. L. accomplishes what he wants, he talks about members of his family as though he could make them present somehow, at least to himself. I think he appreciates it when I listen and ask about details, which, in distance and their absence, look much more important and immediate than the things that used to appear important but that suddenly turned into something less tangible than last year's snow. And so, I suddenly cease to find it strange that someone whom I've never set my eyes on comes to life for me, without the person knowing anything about it or even being alive anymore.

He spent both those days with me, and I had the feeling he was thawing out. He kept staring at me as if I were naked, though I was fully dressed because it is cold in the attic at night. Mr. L.'s mother was a dancer. That's just about all I know of his past. He's never spoken about his father.

Mr. L. told me that his wife had had breast surgery before she left Prague. I asked what it looked like. Very gently, he drew a line around my chest with the pad of his index finger, pointing out the place where the breasts meet the chest and where there was a delicate, extremely delicate filament, the scar from the surgery; the more expensive and skillful the doctor, the thinner that strange little path.

Morning. Twice. A rolling pin. Four times. A cup of mustard. A lightbulb. Ten marks, which I can convert anytime.

November 10. Once. A jar of artificial honey. Twelve marks.

"There are three kinds of people, if you want to make it simple, without wasting your time with minor differences," said Mr. L. as usual, almost greeting me with these words. "First come the referees, who want their truth to be binding for everyone, with no arguments to the contrary. Each argument only complicates matters. The second ones sail toward the shores of India and discover America. They know very well that the world already exists, yet they have to prove that it's true again and again, in order to relate it to their own humble selves. As far as Napoleon is concerned, it never dawned on him that he had disappointed France. France always disappointed Napoleon."

"It was a bit different the last time you spoke about it," I responded.

"It's always different."

Evening. Three times. I had a stomachache. A box of matches. An airmail envelope. Two ounces of sugared jelly.

It struck me, after Mr. L. had left, just how it is between a man and a woman. Men are bored without women, and then again with women. The mutual attraction that exists between men and women also contains the source of their mutual irritation. This applies to men as well as to women, but it's not exactly the same for women as for men. Mr. L. is not the only one who mostly wants it just so, the way he says he wants it. Ludmila too is obsessed by it, the other way around, or upside down.

* * *

Old man O. talked about Africa in periods of drought and hunger. He lay next to me like a lamb, clothed from head to toe, without trying so much as to touch me. He touches me with his eyes only. Incredible things must take place in his head and heart, and I know I am part of them. Does he, through me, conjure up all the women he has ever loved, betrayed, and left, or who betrayed and left him? Or the women and girls with whom he was happy and who reminisce about him to this day? What happened to them? Why is he so alone and why does he never talk about it, telling me instead about some mysterious travels through the African continent while he gazes at me as though gazing at all those past women. And not just women in the sense of lovers but also women whom he had painted, before his nails and fingers were scorched off. Old man O. keeps staring at my mouth, too, and I can just imagine what kind of thoughts go through his mind, and he also stares at my eyes, face, forehead, hair, and legs.

"How come you've never had any children?" I asked.

"They would have hated me for helping them into this world," he replied, and smiled.

"That's not true. Children never blame their parents for what their parents can't help. It never occurred to me to blame my father because there is a Hitler."

He lay next to me all night long. I too didn't feel like touching him. I was thinking of a number of other things. Then I imagined myself old, like old man O. Finally I imagined how starving giraffes crossed the river Niger.

Mr. L. brought some news from the front and left a list of verdicts with me, as submitted for approval by court officials to the Jewish Government Council. Rosa

Hirsch was given ten days for picking up an extra lunch with a food coupon she found, and Felix Wolf got fourteen days for falsifying a food coupon and also picking up and eating an extra lunch. Mr. Abel Schulholf received three weeks for luring the people in the Old Age Home into giving him their food under the false promise that he would bring back something better, much more palatable to them. Mancie Breier will take a fourteen-day rest for thirty pounds of stolen potatoes, and Elisa Severin got three months in the cooler for stealing a package from the post office. Jonas de Vries got two days of jail for lifting a slab of wood at the railroad station. In addition, the band is looking for a trumpet player. I would be surprised if they haven't found one already.

Yesterday Ludmila wanted to know whether it was true that Harychek Geduld is a communist.

"I don't really know," I replied. "Who wouldn't believe in something besides the coming of spring, summer, fall, or winter?" I smiled. It also occurs to me that Harychek Geduld acts at times as if he and his gang know something that no one else knows.

My father, from what I can remember, was always upset when people promised something was true that could be true at most for a couple of weeks or months, if they were lucky.

"He's puffed up like a balloon that's about to burst," said Lida, as if guessing what was on my mind. "He thinks that just because he thinks differently, he is different, as if, unlike others, he didn't have the same nose between his eyes, two arms, a body, and two legs, and as if the rest of them were afflicted with some kind of invisible leprosy."

"One communist I know traded his three rations of

bread and sugar for a Russian textbook," I said. "Most likely, he also believes that along with morning, noon, and night, every clock tower can announce dawn or sunset or whatever else."

"Do you mean to say that they're insane? I'd be surprised if Harychek Geduld was capable of such a thing. I'll be watching to see just when it evaporates from his head. Craziness should be measured by how much courage one is left with; that would do, as far as I am concerned," Ludmila said rather dejectedly. Then she said, "For some, it's enough to arm themselves with some idea, like the insane. I'd be content with just knowing for a fact, morning, noon, and night, what's important for me and what isn't, and what's important in general and what isn't, if you know what I mean. Because otherwise everything is ridiculous. You ought to be glad that you can hear the striking of the clock tower and have an idea what time it is, whether it's time to eat or time to go to sleep."

"I don't know," I said. "All people who are obsessed with an idea are capable of sacrificing others, above all those who disagree with them. I know from Mr. L. that the Zionists in the administration think that for the Promised Land of the future, it is crucial to preserve as many young people in the best possible condition, people who will have the strength even after this war to go, hoe and shovel in hand, to dig in the desert, seeking water in the rocks. So instead of the young, the middle-aged and old people go off, and all they can do is have their eyes filled with reproach. The communists, on the other hand, think that the revolutions of the future will be justified if, instead of themselves, they send all those to the east who still have not joined them. Otherwise, who would be left to carry out such a revolution?"

"In the end, isn't it better for the old, the weak, or the weary to board a train to the east and get it over with, before they're completely worn out?" asked Ludmila.

"As far as I know, they convene a meeting before each revolution; therefore no one needs to fear that it might arrive too quickly."

I offered some of my food to her. Ludmila was embarrassed to start eating immediately, as if the time it took was somehow significant.

Once. A vial of aspirin. Fifty marks. Two dish towels. A watch.

In the evening Ludmila came by again and I asked her whether Harychek Geduld was still on her mind. She was neither nervous nor upset that I had let her wait downstairs for so long a time.

I gave her a collection of rabbinical wisdoms that I had just been given and for which, in any case, I had no particularly strong need. Incidentally, I doubt Ludmila will try and tackle it in the foreseeable future.

She talked about a German poet who converted and who had supposedly wooed an executioner's daughter, and I wondered why she dragged this out, as if she wanted to tell me something else. I asked her if she could date an executioner's son, if things were to come to that.

But what she was interested in much more than Harychek's ideas about how to destroy the world—which, incidentally, needn't be of such concern to him, since it's of such great concern to so many others—was the sum of the experiences about which he had spoken.

When he was younger, before they left Prague, he had visited one of his aunts. He'd spent the night there. He had all kinds of dreams, about women and girls on his street. All of a sudden, he'd felt a kind of nervousness that he'd never felt before. Something frightened him and he had no way of expressing what that was. But the thing that frightened him was at the same time quite pleasant. When he woke up, he'd felt some dampness in his loins. No one had ever told him that that could happen and that it would come by itself. In the end, he guessed, of course. It was strange, pleasant, and a bit painful. Later, he dug out of his aunt's medical book that when a boy or young man gets it for the first time, it hurts slightly, because it "opens afresh."

"That sounds nice, it 'opens afresh,' " said Ludmila. "Did it also say that a woman has to be with a man if she wants to become pregnant?"

She was pleasantly surprised that a boy's body too was in pain when it happened for the first time, just like the body of a woman. But she admitted that it was not an enormous ache, it was just a fright and the residue of a slight pain, like an echo slowly waning. She thought about its being beauty and pain together, like sister and brother. And when she considered that Jewish boys must also bleed when a piece of their skin is removed according to the old ritual, on the eighth day after their birth, some of the fear that she had of her own body dwindled away, God only knows why.

"For everything that's good or at least better than thoroughly rotten in me, I give credit to my mother," said Lida. "For instance, the fact that I'm still healthy while she's probably dead by now. And that it gets more intense, the more time that passes since she was taken away. Though I'm afraid that one day it will be so intense that I won't be able to bear it."

Then she turned her thoughts to Geduld, saying, "You know, children of rich people should be humbler

than children of poor people. They should know that a
price must be paid for each injustice, don't you think?"

"Here too?"

"Here especially," replied Ludmila.

"But why should children pay for every injustice?" I
wanted to know.

We watched through my garret skylight as some
boys from the local Home for Wayward Children stole
hand luggage from some of the people who had just
arrived from Copenhagen, Berlin, and Amsterdam. As
she watches Lida feels omniscient. People who have
just arrived and passed through the German treatment,
in most instances for the first time, lose all caution,
under the impression that they will be able to hold
onto whatever was not taken by the Nazis before they
set out on the transport. As though everything they
had experienced at the hands of the German officials
and soldiers was unique, they begin to feel as if they
are somehow past danger after their arrival, what with
Jewish officials and policemen around. This is the moment when the local people steal whatever the new ar-
rivals aren't holding or haven't tied to their wrists. For
the most brazen boys from the Home, the decisive
thing is how a suitcase looks, as if the appearance of
the luggage determined its content. I won't ever take
my best suitcase with me into a transport east, I keep
repeating to myself. The more cautious thieves steal
those suitcases and bags that are closest to the exits. If
a transport has older people in it, it's sometimes
enough to go and ask for the bag they're carrying in
their hands, because quite a few of them think that the
kids are porters, like at a railroad station. Lida and I
try to guess by the appearance of the bags at which

particular moment their owners will lose them.

During the second stage, we watch as some of the boys disappear with their loot into the houses on the next street over; from there, through passageways in the courtyards, they proceed, rather slowly, as if that piece of luggage in their hands had always been theirs, even though they're probably dying to find out what's inside and what will come in handy. In the end, no one cares to whom the piece of luggage belongs. When you know who, what, and how, all the pros and cons emerge, like shadows. And questions are always uncomfortable.

The affected parties first discover what has happened at the registration tables, where something like customs control for contraband tobacco, alcohol, jewelry, and money of every sort takes place. Instead of their bag, they receive a registration number and a card. And so, just when they think that the worst is over, they lose the rest of their belongings, standing stupefied, as if their clothes have been taken right off their backs. Some stand transfixed, as if they can't believe their own eyes. Some weep.

"Mr. L.," I remarked, "once told me that wolves are not afraid of dogs, but dislike their bark."

We went to look at the insane asylum, a place Lida and I are most fond of going to. One of Lida's acquaintances is there, Melissa F. She was brought to Theresienstadt from Greece. Her mother is a Jew from M., where her father owned a transit company with two buses and twelve taxicabs. Melissa's father had a stroke when his bags were stolen in the local quarantine, and her mother was subsequently sent to a different barracks than Melissa.

Melissa's mother was the most beautiful woman we

had ever seen. She went away right after the ashes of
their papa had been taken to the local columbarium and
Melissa had gone crazy.

I noticed on several occasions that it is possible to talk
normally with Melissa. She also looks as pretty as a
picture, only she is scared for no reason and glances
around all the time. Once, she had some remnants of
food on her lips. For the longest time I couldn't understand why she was in the mental hospital, until I tried
to shake her hand once. No one must touch her. Other
times, she might burst out at you for no reason, like a
cat. Still, she is always dressed up nicely. You can certainly see that she is well brought up.

She told us again how lonely she feels even with other
people around and how she would like to get married
and have children. Lida—as fond as she is of her—says
Melissa only pretends to like people. She probably
doesn't even like herself. Her hair has begun to turn
gray. She has beautiful chestnut-colored hair. She is
supposed to have slept alongside her mother till the very
last day.

I had the feeling that Melissa F. was gaping at us, as
if at our place she was seeing a house, a garden, and in
the garden, a cradle with an infant in it whom she held
up to her breasts to nurse. Then she stopped noticing us,
peering, as if on the lookout for someone who was just
about to arrive. She seemed, through us, to be having a
conversation with her husband. She behaved as if someone had come within a step of her, hugging her and the
baby, kissing their lips and in the end remaining there
snuggling up to them.

Then she gazed into her arms, as if holding an infant.
She opened her lips. Perhaps she spoke about how much
weight the baby had gained. And about how she fed him

and how she changed him. Then she reached for herself with the palm of her hand, the way mothers do when they want to see how much milk they have. She smiled blissfully. It was a gentle smile, like a whiff of wind or a rustle of leaves. Melissa's eyes were glowing like two mirrors reflecting the smile of the baby who had never been there.

Lida clasped her mouth. Melissa wouldn't stop smiling, as though she was hearing a voice telling her she had a reason to smile, like all women who are happy.

On our way out, a doctor told us that Melissa would leave on the next day's transport to the east, along with two thousand of the mentally ill.

"Someone took it into his head that gypsies would be done away with on Monday, Jews on Tuesday, the Zulus from Africa on Wednesday, and Americans on Thursday. And neither you nor I are the least bit surprised," said Lida, "because it belongs to the normal course of things, just as much as the fact that the earth turns or that the sun rises and sets again."

Then she said, "When I hear such news, the first thing I do is look around to see how far I am from the event, and only after that do I think of anything else."

Finally she said, as if she were actually interested in my reply, "I used to think that it wasn't even possible to finish off all the people of a particular kind, like, say, the gypsies, or the Jews, or some other group, such as the wandering Yugoslav traders who used to walk up and down our street in Prague with their shops tied over their shoulders, selling a nickel-apiece combs, knives, prophylactic rubbers, and the cheapest perfumes I'd ever seen."

I knew perfectly well that she was getting at something else, and she finally said that she had had a dream

in which she lay on a mattress in my garret and someone
came over, wanting what they most often want from me.
It occurred to me that it was weighing on her mind that
my straw mattress was more fully stuffed than hers. I
also don't change it as often as Ludmila does. My straw
mattress is long, wide, and thick. And most of all, it
doesn't smell of ammonia, like most of the straw mat-
tresses around here.

"Aren't you ever afraid that you'll get sick from it?"
asked Lida at last.

"So far I haven't either become sick or died," I answered.

"But what if you were to get a cramp or become
frightened right in the middle?" she said at last. "I'm
terror-stricken just thinking that it involves your teeth."

But this wasn't exactly what Lida wanted to hear
either. Sometimes I find pleasure in alarming or dis-
couraging her, as if I knew that it made her sick to her
stomach. I already told her once that it was just a reflection of my own feelings. What really scares Ludmila is
that she will be sent away to the east, knowing only what
I'll have told her about it. Or that it's all predetermined
in people, from the beginning to the end, as if an old
man or woman were already contained in the infant, the
adolescent contained in the child, a mark of death sown
into each quiver of life. But just because it is predetermined, it doesn't mean that one will necessarily survive
it. I know for myself just how many things there are that
a person wants without ever being able to get and how
many things there are that a person wants to understand
without ever being able to grasp. It's as if Ludmila were
saying through her many words, "I am innocent, but I
don't want to be."

I never told her what it's really like, that it's always

the same but also always different. Am I to explain to her what it feels like when I have nothing to eat and, again, when I'm full? How you begin to feel that it assumes some strangely familiar life, as if a blocked flow of blood were gushing against me, and as if everything, the mouth, the tongue, and the teeth were living its very own life? Or that my mouth is sometimes quite sore?

Only it's sometimes sweeter and purer when I can tell myself that it's exactly what I want.

Or am I to tell her that for a fraction of a second I daydream about how I'd like to be a man, wishing to feel as good and be as firm, and how pleasant it would be if someone were to be with me in just the same way?

"We're still young," Ludmila says, "I don't want to die."

"You know yourself how often you prepare a rope to hang yourself, only to end up drying your petticoats on it," I said.

"I don't want to die before I live through everything a person is supposed to live through," said Lida.

"It seems that just as people have to pay for courage, they have to pay for fear. And there isn't all that much difference between renouncing something and treating yourself to it."

"I'm still a virgin," said Ludmila.

"Be glad that no one has raped you yet."

"I had a dream where that happened. Or actually, I don't know what happened exactly."

"In any case, we're both living terribly fast," I said.

"I can understand all children who will never be born," said Ludmila. Then she said that I was looking good enough to be able to do anything I wanted with my body. "But I don't want to cry about it on the street."

Once, Lida tried to explain to me what it is that

comes over her. She can feel it charging at her like
some touchable shadow. She never knows where it
comes from. In the last few weeks, it has been coming
more and more often. A dull taste in her mouth, the
feeling that everything is dying or coming to an end,
slowly but ever so surely. And even though people
know there's a way out of it if they would only budge,
no one budges. As though it were a room with no doors
and no windows.

"What did you dream about?" I asked.

And then, "Was he a German?"

"Maybe he was a German," replied Ludmila. "Later
I tried to imagine it again. The scream, the horror, the
motion of the hand toward the groin, and the fainting.
I went with that painter whose fingers were mutilated at
the Little Fortress. But you weren't around anymore.
You went away in the same railroad car that Milena'd
gone away in. And that's how we discovered that they
were the same railroad cars, traveling back and forth to
the east, again and again." Then she said she let it fall
out of her mouth because she didn't want to choke on
the blood.

"You are mad," I said. "You'd never do such a
thing."

"Maybe I'm afraid of life, not of death," said Ludmila.

"I doubt that you'd want someone to bleed to death
because of you," I said.

November 12. Once. A jar of homemade caramel.
Twice. A bouillon cube. A bar of soap. Five times in the

evening. A pencil. A raw cucumber. A letter opener, as sharp as a dagger.

November 13. Six times. Ten grams of black rye bread. A half-kilo bag of coarse-grained flour. Caraway seeds. Salt. An ounce of margarine. A quarter of a kilo of powdered sugar.

November 14. I dreamed again about the Luftwaffe officer. It was almost as if I wanted to dream about him. I was envious of Ludmila's dreams. Or maybe it was something else.

He appeared at my attic, standing between the stairway and the door that I had specially left open till someone came. He was elegant, frozen to the bone, and purple in the face, wearing a blue cloth coat with a wide belt and touching his aviator knife with his hand. He was standing in front of me, his right arm folded at his hip and his hand closed in a relaxed fist. He didn't have to tell me he probably liked to be photographed like this. The uniform suited him. All three silver buttons were fastened, the Iron Cross attached under his left breast pocket. Above all this he wore his little Luftwaffe wings.

"My personal sword maker in Sauerland on the Rhine made this dagger for me. Have you ever heard about that Prussian country, about the city of Solingen? He forged it from the output of a mine not far from here, from the ore reserves in the Iron Mountain."

A while went by before he took off his hat. He had fair, almost white or platinum-colored, hair, soft like a woman's, blue intelligent eyes a bit cool for my taste, and extremely sharply etched features. He was tall and slender. He moved without constraint, effortlessly, as though he had been used to giving orders and expressing his desires since childhood, expecting no objections.

"Come over here," he said. "Perla S.?" He peered at me, as if to say, A Jewish whore. Who would have thought. A Jewish whore.

I know exactly what he wants: He wants me to help him take off his coat, or rather that he help me help him take off his coat, and afterward he just wants me to take care of him from beginning to end.

In addition to numbers, all women had to add Sara to their names, and all the men, Israel. Sara in Hebrew means "princess." That means all Jewish women are of royal blood.

Once, I had been on the lookout for him for a long time before I finally saw him taking a shortcut through the park on his way from the Casino, which is off limits for our people but from which nice dance music can be heard. Later he said that the music was composed by Peter Kreuder but that it was still full of foreign elements. He intimated whose fault that was. And he racked his brain about how it was possible that people who, in his opinion, had made a bad deal with history —who, as someone had said, could neither live nor die, like an ailing old man—seemed to continue to have such an influence on music, literature, and the law, even though they didn't exist anymore.

I know that many Jewish girls and boys dream about having acquaintances in the Gestapo or about being in the Gestapo themselves, officers, commandants, wearing

German uniforms, good shoes, warm cloth overcoats, fur gloves made of real sealskin and real hamster and rabbit. I have often dreamed that I was a German Breadbasket lady, one of those people who go into the ghettos on raiding inspections, making off with whatever they manage to pick up, even if it is Jewish property, and when they find money, well, I have never seen or heard about a single Breadbasket lady who would shy away from touching it. However, in my dream I was a Breadbasket lady and a gentleman; I never took anything from anybody. I examined the belongings of old Jewish women and of children who were more helpless than people like myself or like the adults who worked and received ration coupons, so that their stomachs didn't growl from morning till night and from dusk till dawn. And even though I couldn't give them my own sandwich, I never made off with anything of theirs. For this, they gave me looks that were more appreciative than those of Greta Garbo in *Grand Hotel,* which I remembered from the days when we were still allowed to go to the movie houses to see the best American movies. I began to guess the difference between being a Jew and being a German. It occurred to me how I would behave if I had been born a German girl.

He asked me, almost as Ludmila did, what it tastes like. He was not the first man who wanted it that way, asking me afterward what it tasted like. I suggested that taste didn't really enter into it; it was something else and always different besides. He told me about one of those racial institutions that he had looked into on my behalf. He stayed there for a few days to see what was going on, and I was surprised to learn that there weren't just women and girls there but men also. As far as the men were concerned, they not only had their heads measured but also had their weight, size, and literally everything else checked over. He insisted that there was still hope for me, but I had to be patient.

He described what he had observed when he was peeking as if through a porthole into a cabin, from a spot from which no one would have imagined it was possible to watch the people being tested and measured. He added that some institutions had only a select number of women and men, while others had three doctors and three ideological officers for each male or female charge.

But I understood that it was just a promise that he dangled in front of me, like inviting me to some future feast that would never take place.

I'm not so sure I would really want to match all the requirements of the pure Aryan race, possess measurements matching the Nordic skull, its chemical composition of hair, thickness of lips, and its mouth size from corner to corner; at the same time, I can't help but be proud sometimes for having been born with such a close approximation of those requirements. It is as unflattering in one way as it is flattering to me in another.

But my officer repeated that I could still be considered, and if I had some patience and a bit of luck, all was not yet lost. It has occurred to me how he would look if he had been born one of us.

"Aren't you cold in here?" I asked him.

In my mind I can just see a group of German doctors studying the properties of the purest race in test tubes or in milk or vinegar bottles. As old man O. says, they have that instead of a kino palace. It's too bad that we'll never make it into such a clinic, except by way of a test tube, as the representatives of the lowest race. I would particularly like to see Ludmila's face when she got there.

Although all this affects us only indirectly and remotely, something like the relationship of a sound to its echo, it is for us too a picture that foreshadows future generations. The history of the immaculate race, born while we, the insects of humanity still infect the air, will, in some one to three hundred years, take on the appearance that the possessors of pure, Germanic blood discern already in their veins. And just as the pure-blooded German kings constituted the majority among European kings over the last two thousand years, so they'll again rule all over the world, as easily as playing Ping-Pong.

Maybe they really have been the master race over most of the past. Do they hear the echoes of something I myself can't hear, and no one but they can hear? But how can they possibly convince someone who is as far removed as Mr. L., old man O., Ludmila, or I myself, my father, and my mother that they are the elect? The Cabalist says that a king whom no one around him recognized as a king is in fact no king, even if he puts a five-tiered crown made of gold, silver, and precious stones on his head.

"It's not exactly warm in here," he replied, "but that's no problem."

He wanted once again what he had wanted right from the start, even before he sat down on my mattress. He again said what a beautiful mouth I had and how obsessed he was with it, though it was different with me. He claimed he could get away with anything he wanted, within the walls of the fortress. I knew that he could do whatever he wanted, nothing was forbidden him, as long as no German witnesses were around.

It's set apart from guilt, apart from shame, as if we were mere shadows, stepped over by people, but at the same time marked off by location, shape, and size. It's

both the same and different from when he, while flying
on the Eastern Front or in the west, loses what in earlier
times was called his conscience. Adolf Hitler wrote that
conscience was a mere Jewish invention that cripples the
human character, just as circumcision cripples the body.

"It's your people who are the first to prohibit what
they really most desire," he said.

It reminded him of the times when all people were
divided into slaves and masters, but it is something else
as well. It involves only some things from such a past,
if I understand him correctly.

It occurs to me that the rat with whom I live has no
difficulty either. It's merely fearful, hungry, wanting
something or not wanting anything. It has just come to
me that rats in Bohemia are called German mice.

And it became clear to me who it is that really prohib-
its what he most desires. And also what that involves.

If I were German, would I do without a conscience?
The officer suddenly broke into a smile. As if he guessed
my thoughts, he said that here he could feel as if he was
living out the story of Adam and Eve, only in reverse,
because for as long as they were in paradise they were
troubled by knowledge, whereas he could only enjoy
knowledge.

It really has nothing to do with lying, because he
might or might not be lying; still, who has the right or
the chance to prove to him that black is not white, that
a knife is not a pencil, blood is not water, prison is not
a playground, or that a bathroom is just a place where
people rinse off dust and sweat? I didn't understand it,
but he didn't explain anything more.

I could see him gaining self-confidence with every
word, feeling more and more at home. It's probably one
of the things for which we envy the Germans, because
it's so natural for them, as if they in fact were born to

be at the top, to win, to conquer others, and to set
themselves up in the world just as they want, as if it were
their right from the beginning. As soon as he's convinced that I'm a louse, a worm, or a criminal, because
a different mother gave birth to me, he'll step on me,
wipe me out, kill me. And why not? Has he wondered
whether I think that it would be better for us if others
were in their shoes, among all those who have never
liked us and never will? It must have occurred to him
that I was careful with my answer, because I was afraid
that he might kill me or have me killed, or that he might
change his mind about the possibility of getting me into
one of the Nordic institutes.

Something occurred to me that I haven't yet told
anyone, not even Ludmila. As far as I can see, everything the officer said involves only him alone.

Why all of a sudden do we all cling to those same
things, as if to some shadow?

It has also occurred to me that in reality I am just
another serf, because I am of course not even remotely
close to anything German. As far as I'm concerned, I can
do whatever I want, though whenever I find a balance
between what is better and worse, I feel, on retracing my
steps, as if I were retracing my steps to the danger or
the kind of balance I knew as a child. However, this
never lasts long and is soon replaced by unfamiliar anx-
ieties, whose origins neither I nor Ludmila know anything about. It's as if a man could wallow in mud, as
when suckling pigs wallow in the muck, and all that's
needed is for him to step under the water, rinse it all off,
and be through with the muck.

"I know you're strong," I said. "But with some other
strength than the one you find in muscles."

I asked him about what it's like in the Casino not far
from my garret, from which I hear music nice enough

for me to think that the world is beautiful, even if not always for me. The Germans like to dance in the glow of moonbeams or candlelight; inside there is old oak furniture, the kind that adorns the banquet halls of German castles, and French and Belgian castles as well, from which some of the pieces of furniture had been brought. The piano is German. The windows are covered with red velvet on the inside, though you can't see it from the outside because of the thickly woven linen of the black blinds used for air raids.

"For a mere floozy, which we have plenty of here, you've got a pretty good head," he said.

He talked about the kinds of chairs that are set around the sides of the hall, where there are mirrors all over the walls and two large pictures, scenes taken from German history. One picture depicts King Henry II of England, who was the first to expel our people, and the other a crusadelike massacre on the Rhine in 1146. He gave me an explanation of the content and significance of those two pictures, though I could have easily guessed them, and then he asked, "Could you ever think of the female body as a weapon?"

"You already asked me that the other day," I responded without really replying. "But that's when you said you would come back in a week at the latest." I saw what this aroused in him. He looked at me without saying a word.

Then he noticed the black covers and the notepaper covered with writing. All at once, without a word being spoken, I saw that writing a diary could be as dangerous as what is referred to as high treason or as that which is offensive to people having absolute authority over everything that is animate, inanimate, written, or thought up by men.

I had a similar dream about him last week, but I

dreamed then that he came for the sole purpose of finding out who was printing the little pamphlets on badly yellowed paper that have come into my hands a few times recently. But I was unable to satisfy him because I never saw any of the people who were doing it. To this he said that not to know was always more comfortable than to know. And he remarked that I had nice lips. Then he said, like Mr. L., that I had nice hips. He had talked about my legs back when he found the way into my garret the second time, on September 2. I was waiting for him to go further or deeper, but he just said that I had a nice throat.

"Throat?" I repeated. I touched my neck with the tips of my fingers.

He spoke about extenuating circumstances and why people had to renounce one thing if they wanted to achieve another. My appearance, he added, was an extenuating circumstance in my case, and it crossed my mind that I actually never wanted anything more from myself than to sell myself as best I could. He got dressed by himself, slowly, and he left, looking as elegant as when he'd arrived.

The rest of the night I dreamed a single sentence. I kept repeating it to myself, hoping to twist it around after a few times, to shuffle the words and eventually to discover a more flattering meaning, but in vain.

November 15. Once. A red mesh bag. Three times. A can opener. A silver screw-on pencil. A horseshoe for good luck. Five times. A fountain pen. A white silk scarf. Five raw potatoes. A walnut. A clothes brush.

November 16. Twice. A candle and matches. A hair net.
A box of dry alcohol. Three times. A quarter of a loaf
of rye bread. An ounce of margarine. A thermometer. A
tin button. A liter-sized thermos.

Old man O. accompanied Ludmila and me to the Fire
House. We went to the cabaret in the loft where they
were doing *Fledermaus* with Mr. and Mrs. Hofer from
Vienna. We wore dark clothes and felt almost as if we
were in Prague. Old man O. escorted us the way he
would escort his two daughters, two mistresses, or two
friends; and I could just imagine how he must have
carried himself through the far corners of Europe when
it was still permitted. People noticed us, said hello to
him. He answered with a broad smile, as if the mere fact
that there were two of us with him meant a great deal,
the difference between Mont Blanc and Mount Everest,
and it occurred to me that I might rather like being in
his shoes, if just for a moment.

Milena was walking on the other side of the street,
and when she noticed us, she shouted, "If I were you,
I'd never let anyone tell me again that I was old!"

Old man O. must not have heard so well or didn't
allow himself to think that it was meant for him; in any
case, he glanced at me, then at Ludmila, and with
the shining eyes of a man reminded of something
while escorting two young ladies down a sidewalk, he
hoarsely asked Milena whether she wished to say
something.

"No one should dare tell you ever again that you're
old!" Milena repeated.

Old man O. probably felt as never before. But all at
once, something crossed his mind and he gave his *Fleder-*
maus ticket to Milena. I promised to tell him about the

performance. He said he had already seen and heard *Fledermaus.*

Ludmila told me again, "It's so awful, even the thought of it. And the way you put it, then when it ends."

"Why do you keep thinking about it the way people think about sins that they themselves don't commit but that are close to them just by virtue of their renouncing them so passionately?" I asked. Then I mentioned that somehow it always comes down to that.

"Who knows why they want that?" remarked Lida. "Who knows what comes over them?"

"That's just part of the mystery," I said. "It might very well be their revenge for having had to suck long ago and for having been so dependent on it. I have no idea. It must be a perversion. But you can get used to it and then it's not so awful. It's just one of those things."

"Like gelatin?"

"Almost."

"What does it taste like?"

"It has no taste. It's something else."

"You said it's like when you catch a cold, getting some mucus in your chest."

"Sometimes I think it's as if a tree could eat its own roots. Or like when a drop of resin flows out of the bark of a full-grown tree. There's mystery in it, even though it's self-evident and not remote the first time you do it. You feel as if you're learning to get used to it long before you even actually do it."

A refrain resounded in Lida, how is it that it becomes ever purer and perhaps even sweeter in the end. "The only important thing that really matters at just that instant," I said, "is at the same time the cause of my growing a little bit. I feel a quiver and I ask, did I cause this quiver?

"You've never thrown up?"

"If that's the way you talk about it, no wonder you find it deplorable," I said. "It may well be like that if you have to force yourself to do it and need so much strength. But why not remind yourself instead that what is best is what you yourself want to do, for whatever reason."

But I was thinking that it all might change and that when I have to go without breakfast, I find the whole world unappealing and shrunken, small, not glorious at all.

"Would you want that if you were a man?" asked Lida at last.

"You think long and hard about your sins way before you do them," I replied.

Mr. L. got his hands on a German list regarding a shipment of horses, cattle, and pigs and an inventory of goats, sheep, and rabbits, which are now in the Sheep Pen in the care of our girls. It was drawn up by the commander of the security police, Mr. SS Standartenführer Horst Böhme.

Mr. L. read it from the bottom up and from the top down, again and again, maybe a hundred times.

"Is something wrong?" I asked.

He handed me the list. I inspected it.

"Burn it," he said.

"Are they all like this?" I asked.

"Such pedants?"

I think I know now what he couldn't figure out.

I. On 9 June 1942 at 19:45 hours SS Gruppenführer
Frank gave an order, by telephone from Berlin, that on

the basis of a decision by the Führer, the village of Lidice was to be razed by burning. Adult males were to be shot, women sent to concentration camps, and children provided with appropriate education.

The following was carried out:

1. The village was initially surrounded by one unit of police guards.

2. This unit was replaced during the night with 200 men of the Wehrmacht from the reserve brigade in Slané. The police guards arrested all the inhabitants and assembled them first in the village.

3. Women and children, that is, 198 women and 98 children, were trucked to a school gymnasium in Kladno. There they were guarded by the military police division of the *Oberlandrat* at Kladno.

4. After the arrival of two additional units of police guards from Prague, cattle, grain, agricultural machinery, bicycles, sewing machines, and other valuable consumer goods were assembled and transported from the village as follows: 32 horses, 167 head of cattle, 150 pigs, 144 goats, 16 sheep, and an as yet undetermined amount of grain and groats, 32 agricultural vehicles, 3 electric motors, 1 circular saw, 1 plow, 3 hand carts, 1 sewing machine (all this deposited on the state farm at Buschtehrad); further, 100 bicycles, 3 motorcycles, 1 small automobile, 3 scales, 1 meat processor, 40 down quilts and 74 pillows, 3 baby carriages, 18 radios, 27 sewing machines, 1 electric washing machine, 96 pairs of men's shoes, 83 pairs of ladies' shoes, and a large amount of foodstuffs and consumer goods (deposited with the state police at Kladno).

   This list was put together by the military police of the Bohemian Protectorate at Kladno, under the command of Citizen of the German Nation Lieutenant-Colonel Vít.

5. At dawn the arrested adult males were checked against the village registry. The 173 men were shot immediately after by one of the police guard units in a designated place in the ratio 1/2/20.

6. When the village was fully cleared, a fire was set, for which 200 liters of gasoline were made available by the Wehrmacht. The additional amount of 300 liters of gasoline and 200 liters of petroleum, as needed, was supplied by the Gestapo.

7. Appropriate fire-fighting police officers from the regulatory police headquarters in Prague were given detailed instructions as to how to feed the fires, subsequent to which the first house was set afire on 10 June 1942 at 0700 hours. By 1000 hours all the buildings in the village were in flames.

8. On 11 June 1942 a division of Jews from the Theresienstadt ghetto buried the corpses of the men who were shot in a mass grave in the village.

9. On 11 June 1942 a group of SS trench diggers of 1/1/35 men was sent to blow up those walls that were still standing. This unit did not prove to be sufficient, because, according to some expert opinion, two strong units outfitted with the best equipment would need at least 14 days to perform the task.

10. With a view to securing additional objects of value, such as farm machinery and iron for scrap metal, 3 divisions from the Reich's labor service were sent in and simultaneously utilized as cleanup divisions for the trench diggers.

11. The Lands Administration Office of Prague was ordered to turn the entire arable area into one suitable for agricultural use.

12. The children will be transported on 12 June 1942 in the evening.

13. The arrested women will be sent to concentration camps on 13 June 1942.

   Because only Czech fire-fighting police were available, no firemen were used.

II. Submitted to SS Obergruppenführer Daluege, with the request to take notice.

III. To SS Gruppenführer K. H. Frank.

                                          BÖHME, U.C.

"What does one over two over twenty mean?"

"One commissioned officer, two noncommissioned officers, and twenty policemen," explained Mr. L.

"Were there any of our people there? Someone I know?" I was thinking of old man O.

"One meat processor," said Mr. L.

I could see he wasn't listening to me. I gazed at the strange shadows cast by Mr. L.'s face on the beams, the walls, and the floors. Then I rolled up the report, held it over a candle, and burned it.

November 17. I dreamed again that the Luftwaffe officer entrusted me with the task of finding out who was writing, reproducing, and distributing the pamphlets that urged our people to work more slowly for the war industries of the Reich, because with each killing of an Allied soldier, the end of the war is pushed farther and farther away, just as each Nazi soldier forced to stay behind the front lines brings the end of the war that much closer. In addition, with each German soldier detained here on our account, we save the life of a Russian, English, or American soldier whom he would shoot. It reminds me a little of the way we play Monopoly.

But he didn't look as if the way he was being detained at my place wasn't worth this trade-off. Because with me he feels not the slightest inhibition, none whatsoever, and he looks at the moment as if he were having an epileptic fit. Once for an instant I was petrified that he was going to die, though I was afraid to tell him that, till he himself brought it up.

"In that way we are nearer to death here than at the

front," he said. "Maybe we're just as close when we're falling asleep." Then he showed me where he had been wounded on the left side, stroking the long scar of his stab wound with the palm of his hand.

Briefly, he described how he had gotten it during an emergency landing; they had to take advantage of help offered by some villagers so that he could get to the medics quickly. He claimed that he had been stabbed as he lay unconscious.

"In any case, I wouldn't be the first one to be killed, and I can tell you in advance that I would have to be killed a hundred times, a thousand times, or depending on the group you're using as your yardstick, ten thousand times, if they were to get back the blood that they have lost because of me," he said, in the same voice he had at the beginning of our conversation. He added that it was a case of a wedge knocking out a wedge. And he gestured, as if he could see all those ten thousand ways in just a fraction of a second, so that no words could capture it even if he tried to describe it. But I'm not about to meet him halfway by making an attempt to imagine it and to complete his picture.

Then he told me what he thought I ought to do to be able to deserve my Nordic retraining and with it, perhaps, my very life. The operation was as complex as it was simple, and it wasn't too difficult to undertake it right away. I was supposed to join a group of people at the Prague railroad station, boarding a special car. He warned me not to be concerned about the fate of the people staying behind, because they would literally be of no concern to me. And he mentioned the conditions that might constitute extenuating circumstances, though I discovered some peculiar aspects to these circumstances. The more difficult they are, the more extenuating they will evidently be considered but might not necessarily prove to be.

So I found myself first aboard a train and then, on reaching the harbor, aboard a ship. I was with people who regarded me as one of them, having no idea about my dual face. I was in an invisible relationship with the Luftwaffe officer, who was not there, and I didn't dare feign greater familiarity with the people I was with. I was supposed to feel an obligation to the officer for something that was not even the least bit pleasant. It was as if I had to play a game in which one world worked toward the destruction of another, a part of which still remained, without anyone knowing how to prevent this. And so my desire to sell myself in the world where literally everything was for sale was fulfilled differently than I had originally imagined.

The other end of the world, separated by an ocean, really was the other end of the world. The sea was just as beautiful as Mr. L. had described it. I had a cabin of my own. I was served on board by a steward who taught me English because I didn't want to speak German and he didn't know any Czech. I led a high-class life the whole eight days and nine nights at sea. In the afternoon I basked in the sun, and when the wind was blowing, I had a blanket over my knees, eating tea and cake and watching the waves, the horizon, the flying fish, the sea gulls and the beautiful big birds whose nests were inside invisible rocks or in birch trees on shore. I read a book that, without my knowing or understanding everything in it, gave me a fever. After dinner, which lasted two or three hours, we danced in rooms that looked like palatial halls, with pillars, mirrors, and rich pictures in gold frames, to the accompaniment of music conducted by the bandmaster of the ship. And above the music, like a

great din, we heard the roar of the sea and the still
darker humming of the engines on the lower deck. At
night, the steward escorted me into my cabin, and at
times we gazed at the sea, immense, unknown, and beautiful. I watched a long white wave pass the stern, illuminated by the moon, a furrow behind the ship, a huge
propeller whirling up the sea.

On the seventh evening the captain asked me to dance
with him. He was a tall, slender man of about forty,
resembling my father but every now and then giving me
the feeling that he was the Luftwaffe officer's double.

The ship was called *Death*. I asked him whose idea
it was to christen such a beautiful ship with such a
strange name, but the captain smiled, saying that it was
just a word and I could name my ship any name I
pleased. He said no more about it.

Then, since he wanted to change the topic of our
conversation, we began to talk about demons while we
danced. I never discuss demons with anybody, and if
Ludmila hadn't brought it up once, we would never have
gotten around to it. I spoke to him about Milena. Of all
the girls I was with at L 410, Milena was weird to such
a degree that no one was sorry for her when in 1943 she
departed with an August transport to a Family Camp in
the east. I didn't even know why it was it always came
back to Milena. From what I remember, she never gave
any joy to anybody, as if she thought that somebody
else's joy must always be paid for with her own bitter-
ness.

For the captain, this was of interest and he smiled,
saying that there were people of that sort on every ship.
And that in addition to people whose departure aroused
pity, there were people like Milena, who were pitied by
no one. All of a sudden, I realized—or felt—that Milena

too was a demon. And that each demon had his own preferences, conduct, and tastes. And the ship's name was *Death* to make me see that everything this enormous was death. And that death made people greater than they were while they were alive, as if it were a life turned inside out, only knowable now, as clear as knowing friends from enemies. Death alone could pass the final judgment on everybody, what one really was, and what one was not. And all at once, I had to laugh that I had several times been rumored to have died. And that the same fate awaited the strongest as well as the weakest. And that life was only what was proper and knowable, even if small or modest, and greatness is death.

I danced with the captain for a few minutes after the music stopped, and the captain again smiled at me as before, as if he knew what was going through my head.

"At times I'm obsessed with Milena," I said.

"We're all obsessed with them all from time to time," the captain responded. There was a secret, unspoken agreement between us, and he knew what I meant without my saying it aloud. He had a very deep voice, serious eyes, and when he smiled, lifting the corners of his mouth, I could feel his piercing glance, as if in reality he wasn't smiling, not even a little.

He said again that small as I was, I was much more beautiful than I thought.

Then he said, "My officers and sailors know who's who when it comes to that. Each one of them knows what he does with the woman he is seducing."

I didn't respond to this. It's just as much of a luxury as the luxury of his ship, I thought, to blame someone for what he does and what he is doing thereby to someone.

And so I was thinking about why, because of people

like Milena, some events seem to be bloodier and to come more unexpectedly, replacing one another more precipitously than we seem ready for.

The uniforms of the musicians were similar to those worn by the ship's stewards. All at once, I realized in what language the captain and I were conversing. It was the same language in which the name of the ship was written on the prow and on the stern, painted on every rescue boat, and brightly illuminated over the bar, from which a choice of lemonade or beer was served to the musicians. The ship was sailing smoothly. I ceased to marvel that in such an enormous space, a paltry ship such as this one appeared to be steadily and firmly on its course.

I asked the captain whether he thought about the people the ship was carrying. He answered yes, but not to the degree that he thought about the ship and the rules of navigation that were essential for its safety.

I was thinking that the ship was after all built by people, but, afraid that the captain would tell me the truth, I said instead that I preferred to dance slower dances.

"Some compositions are premiered on board ship," said the captain. He pressed me to him as they played a tango, but when I drew back, the result was that he embraced me more closely.

Suddenly I smiled, but the captain had no idea that I smiled because I had realized that I had my own "weapon," not only against him but against everything that was yet to come. I began to feel that I and those in my group were on the same level as the captain, his officers and crew members, the passengers. And I knew I wouldn't hesitate to use my weapon to keep from being crippled by the rush of coming events. I've been aware of the presence of my "weapon" since I was thirteen, though I know that it might sound trite when you put it into words. At night I dreamed that the captain and I had reversed roles. And the captain must have known while being in my skin that some of the things that I knew I'd have to tell to my Luftwaffe officer.

It ruined my dream about sailing. When I approached the man with a moustache at the harbor on the other side of the ocean, to tell him about my fears, he put his finger to my lips, the palm of his hand on my chest, and against all my expectations, he smiled at me. Shivers ran down my back. I woke up feeling cold.

Once. Twenty-three marks. Some shampoo.

Harychek Geduld has perfected his Monopoly board. The game is now played neither by Jewish rules, where one side gives orders and the other carries them out obediently till its own self-annihilation, nor by Russian, English, or Italian rules, with which Geduld has refurbished the game, making it entertaining and susceptible to all possible variations. Now all the enemies of Germany have been defeated and stamped out, and Harychek Geduld has repainted the squares into German territories, from Alaska through the Urals to the Atlantic coast in France, and the other half of the globe is brown and marked with small swastikas.

Now the Germans are destroying one another within Harychek Geduld's war squares, using the same rules by which they wrought destruction on the entire world during the ten-year war. "Have your skull, sexual organ, and the thickness of your hair measured and then take your place in the square marked 'green eyes.' " When someone rolls a six: "Immediately shoot the black-haired owner of the farm, pick up his blond wife and daughter, and advance ten squares."

Only Geduld's Adolf Hitler is winning; he's the only one left, though he has to return to the start of the game because he has nobody to bake bread for him, sew his clothes, make his shoes, or build a roof over his head. On the first and last squares, Harychek has replaced the little swastikas with question marks.

I drew a card: "Shoot your father for disavowing his Jewish grandmother."

I read it, asking him whether he too hadn't become insane. He wanted to know whether it had ever crossed our minds, as it had his, what that man must have looked like, let's say, some hundred and fifty grandmothers back, when nails had been beaten into him, one into each palm and one into the drawn instep of each foot, when he knew that he was not going to get off those olive-wood boards of his. It occurred to both of us that he must have been scared. Incidentally, I read somewhere that when it reaches that point, fear is greater than God and stronger than all. And it also became clear to me just what kind of fear it must have been. According to Harychek—and not just according to him—we are all of one flesh.

"It's easy to say when you're not one of the chosen race," I said. "I would like to hear what you'd have to say if you'd happened to be born one of them."

"Which carries more weight—when the oppressed want justice or when those who aren't oppressed want justice for everyone?" asked Harychek Geduld.

All his life, Harychek has liked turning things upside down and inside out. As if with such twists he could find more truth than in the things that prayer books or old primers make so nicely digestible.

"I'd like to see how you'd act if you were of German flesh. Or were some other kind of purebred meat. If your blood were as pure as wine. Something of that sort, if you know what I mean. If things were working out for you, just as they are."

Then I asked, "Do you think that all those people were just as scared underneath—the ones I mentally take my hat off to or secretly cheer, no matter where they were born, because they came up with courage where others came up with something else? And if someone saw them up close, would he be shocked at how miserable they looked, with anguished eyes, and hands and knees shaking, so that none of them could see?"

Harychek gave me a long look. I waited for him to say something.

"Did you ever have to look in a mirror just to make sure you were still there?" he asked.

As usual, he had had an argument with Lida, who had accused her own family—meaning in part almost everybody—of going to their execution like sheep. She preferred to play Geduld's original version of Monopoly. At this, Harychek Geduld merely asked why prisoners who were sentenced to long jail terms or to death never, or at least hardly ever, end their lives voluntarily, before the hangman does it for them. No matter what their race, nationality, or the legends connected with individuals or with whole nations might be. He named a couple of examples.

Then he began to paint some new squares on the Monopoly board. When you looked at them all together, you saw a poem of his, this time about how we all hang onto life, tooth and nail, just as everyone before us has hung onto it tooth and nail, just as all those after us will probably still be hanging onto it for ages to come. Then he invited us both to come by in the evening, after dark, because tomorrow, he'd found out confidentially from the Cabalist, a transport was to leave with him on it. We should both show up in the evening when it gets dark.

Once. Two potatoes. Twice. A quarter of a loaf of rye bread. A coupon worth two lunches.

Ludmila and I discussed what the most important thing is for each of us and at what times. Ludmila, to her horror, discovered that for her it changes. Before, it was important that she know that everyone she liked—her parents, grandmother, friends—all were all right and doing fine, and all she needed in order to feel happy was to know that she was liked by others. To this she added her beauty, and this sufficed for her happiness. So long as she didn't harm anybody, it was clear that she was good-natured, never taking on responsibility that was beyond her grasp. Everything that life brought seemed new to her. She felt like a traveler, journeying from one day to the next and from youth to adulthood, collecting new experiences along the way, stashing them away for what was still to come.

But it has changed for me also. It's no longer just my family, girl friends, boyfriends, the cabaret or theater, books, and a bit of wickedness that makes life more adventurous. I'd like to be able to say, as I could have before, that among the most important things for me are a glance at the moon, the stars, and the sky at night; the past, which hides some secret within it, and the future, which is better because it contains hope; the world as it probably is; sleep, because it brings beautiful dreams; and daydreaming, which makes up for everything I have not had.

"I'm afraid of strangers," I said. "Of the dark. Of

being left at the very bottom, all alone, poor, without what my mother called my honor, of being punished and of losing something important, through no fault of my own."

"Do you seriously believe that much in happiness or destiny?"

"I don't know."

"Like you, I'd like to believe that something beautiful is waiting for me. Something unexpected. What you call romance. But I'm afraid I'll get burned. Or that I'll go crazy and look dumb, like people in the insane asylum. Or that I'll waste my life, that nothing that I really want will come to pass. Earlier on I was afraid that I might die. Are you afraid of dying? What are you afraid of?"

I knew that Ludmila wanted to talk about her fear. "I'm afraid of dying all the time," she said. "Of never succeeding at anything. I'm afraid to travel, the way someone else might be afraid of heights." She thought boys were attracted to girls. I told her that it was definitely an instinct but also their ego, big as a church on a town square, the desire for friendship and whatever it fosters. All at once, it seemed to me that Ludmila no longer found funny things funny. I smiled at her.

"Read the rules and regulations the next time you go skating, Lida. When you fall down, try to get back on your feet again as fast as you can."

"I know." Ludmila smiled too. "And don't go so fast. What do you say to boys when they ask you to say something nice?"

"I told someone once that he reminded me of my grandfather, who was a good man," I said with a giggle.

"I would like to know what love is," Ludmila said suddenly. "How much of it is friendship and courage. How much of it is madness, lying, and irresponsibility. Whether it really is the privilege of happy people." She adjusted her blouse, tucking it into her skirt. She was wearing a checked skirt, the one she wore when she came here from the Home for Children at L 410. "I'd like to know just what sort of magic it is. Why people who fall in love are capable of nothing but smiling, while those who get burned and broken look as if they know just what it's about."

"I would never allow anyone to come close to my body," I said. "Only, for God's sake, don't ask what it is that distinguishes love from passion and passion from the glands. It's probably something like the link between fire and warmth. You don't always need fire, but you do need warmth."

"What if you need light?" said Lida suddenly.

"At times I am dead to it. I look alive, but I'm dead. Do you understand what I'm saying?" I smiled again. Ludmila was thinking perhaps of such things as pride, honor, courage, and responsibility. For her, it was the last straw. Why? I have no idea why. Was she thinking of the times when you had to give so much to get back so little? Of fear, crippling everything? Of compassion, helpful to no one? "Maybe it's no worse than being color blind," I said. "Haven't you noticed that people demand to know the truth, but when it comes to these things, they prefer lies?" Is it possible to compare love with a self-consuming fire?

"I don't want to be a mere animal," said Ludmila. "Do you like the night? You told me that at home you used to like the night very much."

"That was at home. When everything was normal. Now I don't like it as much."

"Why?"

"It seems to me that I become a different person at night." I didn't say that some nights I feel as if the end of the world was drawing near, some terrible disaster.

"Back home I could have dreamed that at night even cowards had the semblance of being more courageous, weaklings of being stronger, and those who were ugly of looking a bit nicer. Nowadays, I'm beset by dread when night sets in. And when daylight comes, it's not dispelled as automatically as when you are awakened by the brightly shining sun. I no longer regard darkness as more than just light, the way I did back home."

"As for me, I probably get hypnotized by darkness," said Ludmila.

I was thinking about what it was like when I used to like the night, because I had nothing to be afraid of. Could I really have thought that weaklings would gain strength, and with the strength, courage, and with strength and courage, perhaps hope? Before, I used to look forward to the coming of the night as much as I looked forward to the breaking of day.

"That will change. Everything changes. Except for what doesn't change," I said. "I knew two boys in Prague, at Hagibor, both of them guitarists. They came here with their guitars. Now they're gone again, with their guitars. Their voices were wonderful. Their playing and singing were really good. If you listened to them, they seemed to be perfect. But as soon as they stopped, they were the most obnoxious kids you could ever imagine. They were always like that. There wasn't much they had to offer anybody, except when they played their guitars and sang."

It seems to me that for Ludmila, darkness is something like what sand is for an ostrich. Old man O. told me that an ostrich lives twenty-five years. That's a lot for a bird like that. What about people? But I can imagine what Ludmila must feel like. Old man O. also said that in the sea there lives a big she-fish with a tiny male, whom she feeds because he is so tiny and whose only

responsibility is to fertilize the fish-mother in return. He
is with her all his life, slowly growing ever smaller until
he perishes, while the fish-mother goes on living. Old
man O. spoke about it as if he wanted to condemn the
way some men want to live. He didn't like it. I held
Ludmila's hand. It felt cold, as if she hadn't slept or
eaten much. But today I cannot help her.

I am thinking of dreams. Lida dreamt that her breasts
were overflowing with milk, and that Harychek Geduld
was saying to her, "I will help you." She knew that he
understood.

November 18. Once. Two potatoes.

Twice. A quarter of a rye bread. Food stamps for two
lunches.

I reminded old man O. of his promise to tell me about
Mexico. He lay next to me for an hour, silently, as if
someone had cut out his tongue; I was afraid he might
have grown mute. Then he described an inlet along the
coast of the Pacific Ocean and the cabin close by he had
lived in, where dogs would jump on the roof while he
slept and roosters crow all night long. He told me about
the colors and sounds. About the lizards in the tropical
port nearby, which start running from the shore into the
sea so fast that they stay above the water, as if running
on their hind legs, halfway to the inlet, until the surface
breaks beneath them at last and they swim away. He
began telling me about the palace made of white marble

that is sinking into the mud and will disappear one day as if it never existed.

Then he talked about the town. I was taken aback because he said that when the Spanish conquerors came, they didn't find a living soul; the inhabitants had already died out. It is said they organized matches on playing grounds similar to soccer fields, with a stone ring on one side through which the players had to pass a stone ball. Whoever won was sacrificed to the gods. Why, I wanted to know. Who knows, maybe they degenerated, old man O. reckoned. Every society that kills the best and leaves the worst is upside down, exchanging a win for a loss, the good for the bad, the beautiful for the ugly.

As opposed to some people, one can talk about everything with the old man. With others one can't speak about anything.

Then he told me more about the dead city, with its pyramids to the sun and the moon, where an Indian girl pure as a virgin would be sacrificed. They would lead her up the sun pyramid's stairs to the flat little top; they would stab her in the crooks of her arms with cactus prickles so that she would bleed and faint before she was burnt as homage to the sun god.

Old man O. sighed. I sighed too. I changed the subject by asking him about the palace that's disappearing in the mud. It's the palace of beauty, he answered. When he was there, a three-member band of beggars played for the townspeople in the violent afternoon heat in front of the palace—a legless trumpet player, his eight-year-old daughter banging on a drum on which was printed in red letters FORGOTTEN BY FATE, and his six-year-old son producing rhythmic sounds with a little piece of wood against a fish-shaped instrument with a washboard surface. The old man told me he had thrown all his change into their basket; then he added half of his paper money. They didn't smile back or thank him.

We sat quietly, and then I asked for more. This time he described the Mexican bullfights in the deadly Spanish style, but instead of six bulls, as in the capital, they killed only four. That afternoon, in the tropical January heat, two matadors competed with each other, assisted by brothers and cousins. According to the old man, it is a one-sided dance, since the moment the bull enters the ring, he is condemned no matter how smart or courageous or capable he is. A matador stabbed one black bull deep into his lungs and ruby blood poured from his nostrils; then the attendants swept the blood into the sand and two teams of mules hauled the dead bull away.

"Why do people want this?" I asked. The bull, an ancient animal that once used to be stronger than a man, is reaping an ancient harvest, paying for its one-time victories while man is paying for his one-time losses. Nothing will be forfeited as long as the stars are shining, the sea is humming, the wind is blowing, the old man answered. There was a mist of memory in his eyes. He remembered that he had had a ticket for a seat on the shady side, number 11, in the third row. In the fight with the black bull the matador's dance shoe slipped off his foot. The fat picador, his brother, fell off a horse when the bull gored it. The old man had stayed in the Galicia Hotel, and went for *menudo*—tripe soup—to the Canteen of Hope in the mornings.

"How does one say *hope* in Spanish?" I asked.

"Esperanza," he answered. "Are you listening to me?"

"Some things sound splendid," I said, "Canteen of Hope, Galicia Hotel, Forgotten by Fate."

Old man O. saw the Popocatapetl volcano from up close, he saw its snow-covered tip; he trod upon the dust from the lava the volcano had spewed out and that had cooled down long ago. In Mexico he tasted fruit which now he was only dreaming about, as he was dreaming about his work, his lost paintings, the dried-up colors. Food in Mexico never disappointed him, he said. And he grew silent again and I didn't hear a word from him until morning.

November 19. Five times. A man's flannel shirt. Laces for spats. A warm-up suit. Two dozen lady's handkerchiefs. A Japanese fan.

November 20. Once. A quarter of a loaf of rye bread. Three times. Thirty marks. A gram of margarine. A bag of dried scallions.

November 21. Ludmila waited till the last possible moment to tell me that she had been called up for a transport, and when Mr. L. didn't show up and I couldn't find him myself, I finally saw that Lida's fate was sealed. Everything that has come to pass in my life, even things of the least significance, comes to pass slowly, irrevocably, as if in no hurry. Things may seem like showers bursting from clouds but are really more like a flood brought on by heavy rains. Maybe they've come abruptly, though they appear that way only in retrospect. I can almost see them arrive, as when someone at a station waits for an arriving train, first seeing it in the distance, like a round point, then growing more and more distinct. And these things are always like trains, arriving, waiting for new passengers to come aboard, then departing again.

Whenever something in my life has come to pass that has had inexorable consequences, it has—at least for a while—paralyzed my ability to understand that it was just a minute, an hour, a night, or a couple of days since it happened; then I recover my senses and realize that it is the end of one thing and the beginning of another. It's as if I almost wished that the longest time, a month, a year, or two years, would go by as fast as possible, even if that would put me just a short distance from my own undoing, figuratively speaking as well as in reality. It's like a moving train that we can only board, but never get off.

With Ludmila's departure, the last of the girls with whom I have been here from the start have now left. And only now, knowing that she won't return, do I sense that I understand who and what she was. It seems that I didn't lift a finger to prevent it. Didn't the invisible scale show a grain of gladness on my part? Why? I don't know why.

Once. Five grams of powdered sugar.

During the night, aside from dreaming about giraffes, I dreamed about tranquility. The stars in the night sky were flying in a wedge formation, like wild geese. I heard myself saying in the dream, "The stars are flying south. They are cold. Look, aren't they beautiful?"

When I woke up, I wanted to call the vision back, but I heard somewhere inside me—like an echo—"What am I going to do? What is going to happen to me? What is going to happen to all of us?" Mr. L. says that the world has long since had no use for us, and that no one ever misses anybody. Has it been that way all along or just with us? I feel as if I have lived two lives. As if my soul were a submarine, with many different air locks. As if I owned several souls, a new one for each day, each night, a soul for Sunday, a soul for Monday, a soul for when I am asleep or awake, alone or with somebody. As if my life were some theatrical performance, in which I am both acting and watching myself act. One life is like a show seen by many different spectators. The second life is a secret act but real, a play not yet staged—for which I am still writing my lines.

It is two years since we arrived in Theresienstadt. It was nice when we were all together, even though it was not so great in many other respects. Two years here is like staying fifty or a hundred years someplace else, so much has happened, so many people have disappeared, so many notions gone askew.

At the same time, we all know that there, where the transports go, things are incomparably worse. And so the choice between what is good and bad has been reduced to the choice between what is worse and worst.

Worst are the days when transports are put together. It's enough just to listen to the clerk from Central Registry calling out numbers and names of people, of blocks and lodgings. I feel as if I have shrunk, become smaller than the smallest insect, waiting to see whether my name will be read, called out next by the clerk. And then comes relief, as if you go from freezing cold into some degree of warmth, from hell to some immeasurable safety, for it is not me this time but my neighbor, friend, enemy, mother, father, brother, or sister.

Are we really all alike, as Mr. L. says? Maybe it's just me who is so rotten that I feel a secret, quiet bliss passing through me, because I have eluded it once more, am fortunate in the midst of so much misfortune, am happy in the midst of the bad luck of others. Where does it come from, inside me? Who poured it into me? Where did I pick it up? Could I rid myself of it somehow, if I really wanted to? Aren't the limits that Mr. L. spoke about going to disappear?

I would prefer a hundred times over to be one of the giraffes I dreamed about last night, or one of the dead stars resembling a wild goose, flying south. And yet I've heard of people who traded their transport numbers for someone they cared about. I know of a father who left with a transport as the price for his two little daughters staying behind, after their mother had died of some inflammation of the lymph nodes. I know of a son who went away so that his mother, over seventy, at the end of her life, could stay behind.

Is it the way Mr. L. says, that it is possible to change the conditions in which people live but not man's nature? To what extent can my selfishness grow before it changes into something far different?

I am foul, because I'm glad to be alive even though I understand exactly how all those affected must feel, those who have been selected and are about to leave. And in spite of that, I'm happy, I want to live.

As Mr. L. says, it is the immaculate German world— which everyone has been making concessions to for so long, because it seemed to be so big, getting stronger then, as it still does now—that will swallow up everything and everybody, absolutely everything and everybody and in whose soul our fear becomes strength. It really is a world built on fear and helplessness, not on hope. What can be the future of a world where, when one scrapes off only a few centimeters of dust, fear, the greatest fear man has ever had of man, can be seen, heard, and felt?

In the evening I'll walk to the town square, where the band of Fritzie Weiss plays. When I hear them play and sing, I am never as afraid as in the morning when I wake up. Mr. L. says that the local Ghettoswingers are quite respectable and would do well even in New York, if it came to that. But a band named Promenade, for which Mr. Carlo Taube is responsible, is not bad either. When there's music, even the Café Trio in the coffeehouse near the square, I have a greater desire to believe that all will end well.

Mr. L. kept looking almost enviously at the Luftwaffe officer, concluding that he was a perfect German military man. At night I had a fever.

I kept thinking of Ludmila. I kept thinking about what would happen if I concentrated on her from today on, let's say, for the next fourteen days at high noon? Could she catch my thoughts, like when signals are broadcast by one radio station and received by another? Would it interrupt her thoughts if she were concentrating on something; her sleep, if she were sleeping; or her conversation, if she were speaking with someone just then? Would it reach her in her grave if she has already passed away?

I would like to warm Lida, if thoughts can give warmth; feed her, if they can nourish; revive her, if they have already killed her. I'm probably not alone in having such thoughts. And yet, I know that it will change nothing and that my thoughts will resemble the echo of the fiercest of screams, fading away moment by moment. In the end, I will forget her, or remember her just once in a while.

Twice. An eighth of a loaf of rye bread. Five marks.

Three times. A box of toilet soap. A cashmere scarf. Five marks.

I've gotten a rash.

PART II

My dreams have always been a problem, just like my body, which has overshadowed everything else that's been of any importance to me ever since I was thirteen years old. It goes way back, to Mrs. Erna V., who lived in the same house we lived in when I was little and we were still in Prague. But now she no longer takes off with our flowerpots, armchairs, or my mother's dressing table, but brings us dried vegetables, caramels made from boiled milk and sugar, and small suitcases that can hold all that we need, without exceeding the permitted weight of 50 kilos per person. She gazes at my father as if she regrets that only my mother isn't leaving with us, and she's crying, though I don't know how many of her tears come from her regret that she won't have my father to trade stories with and how many come from all the rest. She is forty years old and good-looking.

Some of my dreams remind me of just how much I like myself and dislike myself at the same time, without knowing why. Maybe what I like about myself most is in reality just my recollection of the little girl I once was.

Until the age of thirteen, I always dreamed something dreadful, and even though I mostly forgot my dreams, the anxiousness remained for a long time, before it gave way to another dream.

After Ludmila found out that I was no longer "original," as it came to be called at L 410, the Home for Children, I was able to convince her that I was better off. Would anyone rather play dominoes with fourteen-year-old little boys? My dreams improved and I began to dream about wild horses in a large meadow. I said farewell to all those feelings of wholeness mixed with incompleteness, and to the growing suspicion that had replaced my peace of mind—that all my former glorious immaculateness was in fact just a prison. What do I need purity for, I asked, if the only result is isolation and sadness?

And when Lida wanted to know what it had been like, I could tell her that it was like a person who watches an egg break, herself, flowing out of the shell and holding on to its walls, like something made of gelatin.

It seems now such a tremendous journey to go back to the time when I first became aware of my body. More than anything else, it was always a source of surprise. To touch myself meant to touch something that wasn't even altogether mine. I remember my bony hands and fingers, searching after something. I asked incessantly: Is this mine? These breasts, are they mine? Why does a woman have what she has—and a man, what makes him a man? Would I be someone else if I didn't have it? Then I gazed at my body as I would at something that would give me pleasure and that I would give pleasure to. And I did things that I didn't understand and my body did things to me which, for a change, my "I" didn't understand. It took a long time before we became friends, my body and my mind. I try to recall the moment when we—my body and my mind—began to comprehend what was what with regard to my body's illogical but probably necessary demands. First came the conflict that my body appeared to be complete, almost ready to have a child, whereas my head was not that far along by a long shot. Added to this came my desire to love someone, often a man I couldn't even like. Much of it was the obscure, beautiful desire that made me sad, but nicely sad. I knew I had to bring my body and mind together before I could start bothering myself again about how pretty I looked to others. But something told me that I would have to do it alone, just my body and me.

Mama didn't allow Papa to come in while I was washing or while she was helping me wash, not since I was twelve years old. Although she never said it, she thought that only lovers and husbands had the right to see daughters in the bathroom, not fathers. Maybe that's one of the reasons why fathers in their weak moments boast to daughters about their past or imagined lovers. There has probably been only one kind of freedom that man could afford with no reservation, almost since the very beginning: the freedom that exists in his mind. It sometimes involves the strangest things. It's a freedom that can be given no voice and, if given a voice, then can't be conveyed.

Of course, it was not as simple as picking up my skates and going ice skating or my swimsuit in the summer and going swimming at the Yellow or Blue Swimming Pool. At times I felt nervous when someone wanted to touch me. I would bristle and become stiff.

I suspect that it sprang from several things that had happened when I was still so young that my parents

made no secret of what they later tried to hide. But it
was the kind of nervousness that never went away completely, even later, when I was close to some boy. In
my mind, I see Mama cringing because Papa wanted to
touch her the way a man touches a woman, and she
didn't want him to. Once, I went to bed a little earlier
than usual, and the rest of the family was in the
kitchen. Mama went to bed early too. Papa went after
her, bent over her, and started to talk in the insistent,
deep voice used by adults at such moments. Poor
Mama, she would die if she knew that I know about it,
was thinking about it, am even writing about it. To his
words, Mama responded, "No, no, leave me alone, you
disgust me!" Papa again said something and Mama repeated, "Go away!" I don't know what Papa must have
done, because all at once Mama jumped out of her bed
and went into the room where my sister and brother
were sleeping. I heard everything though the walls.
Mama slammed the door and Papa had to go into the
kitchen through the room where I was lying, and I
heard Mama repeat, "No, I've already told you, no."
And then again, "You are disgusting! You're repulsive!
Leave me alone! Go away! You ought to be ashamed of
yourself. I'll wake the children!" They struggled with
each other. Mama tripped on the night table. Papa
made a mocking remark. Then left. Mama didn't sleep
in their bed for several nights afterward. Maybe I
should have understood it back then, but I understood
nothing. Now, a long time afterward, I'm able to put it
all together, arriving at a picture that detracts neither
from Mama nor from Papa. I know that my parents
don't represent all men and women; at the same time,
they represent everything that concerns a man and a
woman. I was horrified that day. I hated Mama for

loathing Papa. I thought I took after him, and so would have the same problems as Papa had with Mama. At first I became impatient, and soon after, cold, as if I were doing something because Mama had done it.

But my dreams about wild horses in large meadows in the summer on the fresh, light-green grass, or in the winter, on the snow strewn with impressions of the horses' hooves, pushed away the bad dreams. I told Ludmila that what she had asked me about first came to me while I was taking a bath. And the two, the dreams about horses and my bathing, became a blur in my mind. I remember that as a little girl I read once that a dream about a horse means something else. As girls we ran after everyone that time, questioning aunts, mothers, friends, as well as teachers, about whether they too had ever dreamed that they were riding a horse. Almost everybody we asked had dreamed about it. But nobody knew what it meant. We felt fantastically experienced, snickering on the side.

Horses, meadows, sunny slopes, and then imaginary fights, started by the boys from my school and by unfamiliar young men out of books, newspapers, and films, under the most trying circumstances, all just because of me. They climbed down from the rocks by a thin rope, just so they could see me, blow me a kiss, and then leave again, crossing dizzying heights.

During the next stage of my dream, I underwent a metamorphosis before my very own eyes. With it, I regained my lost balance, was able to be happy and unhappy during the span of one single moment, for no reason. And so I could understand when Ludmila or Milena all of a sudden burst out crying.

I don't know whether those are dreams, but I do know

that there are forces within me that I have not taken advantage of yet and with which I could probably accomplish something. I remember just how many times I felt this way until I turned thirteen, when, as Mama implied, the child becomes a woman.

At times my body feels like a flame that cannot be extinguished. Fortunately, it's an invisible flame, and the things it burns up are also imperceptible. Sometimes I'm so full of energy that I don't even understand where it comes from, because even if I knew more people than just Mr. L. or little Rabbi B., who has been coming to me since last week, or the gypsy-Jewish half-breed Laszlo Berkovich, all of whom take care that I not go hungry, I would not be able to say that I get my fill every day of the week, as much as I would like or need.

It's a different kind of tension and another kind of energy from the others I know. In answer to this, Mr. L. told me that I'm hungry. All right, I'm hungry; of course, everybody's hungry here. But it's not the kind of hunger that goes away by eating a slice of bread. And because both Mr. L. and I know how things stand, his simple sentence about my being hungry is in reality not nearly so simple.

November 28. Once. A kilo of powdered sugar. Five times during the night. A quarter kilo of bread flour. A stamp album. A sewing kit with spools of black and brown thread. Fifteen marks.

Twice. A German-Czech dictionary, *Langenscheidt*'s. Men's handkerchiefs.

November 29. I saw the Luftwaffe officer as he rode by on his horse, his long coat flapping, riding through the clearing in front of the house of the local commandant. He was soon joined by the wife of the commandant. They both rode strong, light-gray horses, and although they didn't ride fast, they looked very good. In any case, I see that he's still here.

When he last visited me, he told me about his inspection trip through the occupied parts of Yugoslavia, where the local people had once brought him a basket containing fish eyes, that is, he thought at first that they were fish eyes, till he found out otherwise.

He smiled, adding that they had later brought him peaches and Bosnia plums in the very same basket. I knew he was telling me this to test me and also to test himself about something that might be called shame.

After a while, they took off in the direction of the Little Fortress, toward the mountains, and I caught a glimpse of the mayor's wife, flushed in the face, big-breasted and well fed, in a beautiful fur coat. The officer had his little aviator sword with him, and instead of a cap, he was wearing a fur hat.

It was still light out when they returned, and I saw him leading the two horses, ruddy from riding in the fresh air, the horses' mouths steaming and the mayor's wife smoothing out her reddish hair. The pilot was courteous and the mayor's wife appreciated it.

Once. An eighth of a loaf of rye bread.
Twice. Eight marks. Ten grams of margarine.

Ludmila said once, "We're all selfish."
"In the end, everybody is selfish, Lida," I agreed. "I would have to think you were crazy if I thought that

selfishness was completely foreign to you. The question is, where do you set the limit for each act of selfishness?"

"What do you mean?" she asked.

"I knew a man who thought about it a great deal. Mr. L. G. Every day he wrote—in his own way—the Ten Commandmants over again. He was full of friendship, but when he got something, he kept it strictly for himself. And he used to say, 'We are all sluts, dear brothers and sisters, ladies and gentlemen, but we must at least know our limits.' "

And another time she told me, "A year ago there was good news about my family. My father had gotten a new job that should have made him affluent enough to let my mother come up to Prague to visit me. I really wanted her to come because she needed a vacation and I needed to get reacquainted with her. You would like her if you met her, and she was nicest of all when my Dad wasn't around her. I think he frightened her because he had a terrible temper. But Mama was a very nice lady. She had a sense of elegance that seemed to linger just beneath her skin, as if she were a princess captured by beggars as a child. She always seemed half regal, half animal. She had a pretty tough life. I wonder what made her marry a man who was mostly an animal? That probably isn't very nice to say."

Probably she needed to say it to someone.

November 30. Whenever I describe the noise of doors being shut, as they were just now, doors as near as the echo of heels tapping down the stairs, I discover again and again that, once I describe it, it's not the same thing anymore. And even though it's not a lie but what really happened, I have to keep on adding and crossing out words, feeling at times that a single contradiction contains more truth than if I piled all the words I know into one big heap. I wonder whether truth is contained in what happened, in what people feel about why it happened, and in what must happen because it has happened before.

It's one of the many things that exist just beneath the surface, understandable only to those who are in the midst of the situation, like fish in water. It's difficult, maybe even impossible, to convey it through a spoken or written account, to make it even somewhat understandable to those who only get it secondhand. A great many things that happened just yesterday are almost incomprehensible today. Like a scream, heard and then fading, before vanishing altogether. Like when I have a conversation with somebody who is from Prague, as I am, and someone born in Berlin stands around listening but misses so much of it; it's as if he could make out the words but not understand a tenth of what they mean.

Along with this, I wondered what it is exactly that makes a person a grown-up. Where exactly is the line that separates childhood from adulthood? It's certainly not just your head, your body, or your age, even though it is also your head, your body, and your age. Ludmila once came up with the idea that it might be the chain of misfortunes that makes people grown-ups. It's the same as when Rabbi B. told me that everyone still alive by December of 1943 will remain alive at somebody else's expense, irrespective of what camp, what prison, or what free country they live in, even if they are still not convinced that this is so.

I had similar discussions with Mr. L., at about the time my parents were going away. He claimed that only older people were being sent, though Papa was hardly forty years old. Mr. L. asked whether he had ever lied to me, and laughed when I replied that everything would have been worse if he hadn't. Even everyone who dies dies at somebody else's expense, the little rabbi claimed.

It has many advantages, this confiding in an all-patient sheet of paper, one-sided though it is. I remember how one night Harychek Geduld sneaked into one of the German warehouses where they keep confiscated books, to get hold of a volume whose name, along with the name of its author, he had written down on a piece of paper and for which he would get some meat from the man who had asked him for it. At the time, the man worked in the butcher shop.

The butcher was in love with a girl I knew, Diana, whom we called von Dubai. She was beautiful, with small breasts and the most symmetrical face you've ever seen, like all those movie stars and actresses who have their pictures printed on matte-finished paper. She was slim, had a pleasant laugh, and was well read. She used to wear a blouse made of blue and white terry cloth, which was the rage here this past summer.

The butcher's name was Joseph Reinisch, and angelic though the two looked together, they always appeared all bruised when they walked down the street—Diana with swollen eyes and her lover with traces of her bites all over him.

All the same, it was a great love, and all the girls from L 410 spoke about them with envy and admiration, which I could well understand.

I learned as early as that evening that he had asked a favor of Harychek Geduld, who had the reputation of being both a well-read person and a thief. He asked him to provide them with *The Merchant of Venice,* in exchange for a properly weighed pound of beef stew. I don't want to go into the fact that it was the first time someone had heard the name of the author, but I do know that Harychek went through hundreds of books before finding William Shakespeare sometime toward morning.

The following day, without being told, Ernie H. delivered a knapsack filled with all sixteen volumes, chewed up by mice, to Reinisch without being asked to do so, just so that people wouldn't say that he was any worse a man than Harychek Geduld. He was simply dissatisfied with how poor and dusty the books looked.

Diana von Dubai is gone and so is Joseph Reinisch. Somebody said that a car killed him even before he arrived at his destination.

Mr. L. told me that when I sleep, I look angelically innocent, with an extremely pure face and a relaxed body, like a doe resting somewhere on a patch of moss. It occurred to me that a man's glance is like an invisible mirror, which he can both gaze through at someone and be reflected in himself.

Then he congratulated me on my seventeenth birthday, and I again had the feeling, as I've had a few times before, that he was hugging me the way he would have hugged one of his two lost children. He can sit for a whole hour on a pillow next to my mattress, waiting for me to wake up. It's possible that I felt even in my sleep that he was staring at me. Maybe he even stroked me, in reality or only in his mind; in any case, I felt his gaze as a touch. It occurred to me that Mr. L. is three times my age. Although he was careful with compliments, he told me that I was perhaps not only the last of what he had had in his life but also the most beautiful. The worst of it was that it didn't sound as if he were lying. Once, he wanted me to try to fall asleep in circumstances about which I am usually careful.

I long ago gave up guessing about what Mr. L. will or won't do, how much longer he may want to continue his visits here, and when he might get over it; I always seem to misjudge it. Even when I was pretty certain on several occasions that he would not come, sure enough, he showed up again.

At times he acts like Nostradamus, the converted Jew who prophesied for so long that the world would be ruled by headless idiots, until it came to pass, though probably not just because he said it would. But Mr. L. remarked that Nostradamus was wrong; the smart ones would be the ones to lose their heads. I don't remember anymore whether old Nostradamus' prophecy was supposed to last four hundred years or if it was four hundred years ago that he made it.

Once, Mr. L. promised that if he were to depart, no matter how rushed it might be, he wouldn't forget to pull my card out of the Central Registry, letting me dispose of it however I might see fit.

Of course, he must know that each live corpse has, at the most, a forty-eight-hour chance to remain invisible, because within the next two or three days, the number of people remaining in Theresienstadt has to be matched one for one with the number of people who have departed. Furthermore, the counting of people goes by rooms, barracks, blocks, and streets, so that Central Registry is always the first one to be kept up to date.

I've become so used to his presence that I miss him when he doesn't show up. I can tell well enough when he's ready to leave, but not precisely why he comes. A

glance, a word, or a sign from him is all I need. When
he is late, after letting me know he's about to come, I
always hope they won't keep him long at headquarters.
At times the officers amuse themselves by seizing people
without passes right off the street and taking them to the
Little Fortress. No one has ever returned from the Little
Fortress. Yet Mr. L. is the first to insist that we have to
pay for everything in this world and that in the final
analysis, nobody gets what he likes most without lifting
a finger for it.

"I hope you'll forgive me for the wrongs I have done
to you," he said.

"I don't think you've done any more to me than what
people do to themselves," I said.

"In the end, we all develop appetites for what we
never knew we had appetites for," he said, smiling.

Then, in the middle of talking about the officers at
headquarters, he began to talk about the Luftwaffe
officer who flies out and back to the front in his single-
wing plane, in the manner of Reinhard Tristan Eugen
Heydrich, the chief of the Gestapo in Prague, who, before he was assassinated, wanted to eliminate even the
slightest mention of his grandmother, Sara, by removing
all inscriptions from her tomb even though she was not
Jewish at all. On his widow's farm, Lina Heydrich em-
ploys teams of young men drawn from the local work
platoons.

I think I blushed at the mention of the Luftwaffe
officer, and I have no idea whether Mr. L. noticed it.

"I once saw him ride his horse up to the Casino and
leave the horse standing tied to a tree in front of the
fountain in the park," I said.

"They are like trees that seem to grow right up to the
heavens," Mr. L. said.

I was glad that the Luftwaffe officer wasn't mentioned again. It was only later, after Mr. L. had left, that it occurred to me that his allusion might have been intended as a hint that I establish contacts that could lead to an eventual trade. Mr. L. vowed to one of the officers at headquarters that for every instance of demonstrably fairer treatment of the population, the officer might, after the war, receive an unequivocal commendation from the Council of Elders. But that wasn't till much later. In the meantime, I'd see the Luftwaffe officer in his hussar fur jacket; he would come and talk about the setup in the east in a manner he had never used before, failing to understand how I could listen without moving a single muscle in my face. Before Mr. L. went away, he spoke often not only about his family but also about his mistresses, who, now that he was nearing his end, stood out in relief, emerging as if from oblivion, as if in the end, no man ought to lose what he has owned, lived through, saw, heard, or touched, whatever the direction life had taken him.

I have a lucky streak with some people. I'd say that it comes from something good within them. It never goes away. It doesn't go away even in the harshest of circumstances. On the contrary, in such circumstances it only stands out. Some people are beautiful. It's not only the symmetry of their face, eyes, hair, nose, or mouth, the build of their body, or the ability to look well. It is inside people, in who and what they are and how it affects others.

The transport on which Mr. L. departed was joined by a prominent prisoner from headquarters, the German sportsman Freddy Hirsch. He was one of the first men to have made no secret of his interest in his own rather than in the opposite sex. He was one of the finest and also one of the handsomest of men, and several girls sought to win his favor, but to no avail in that respect, though as a companion he was always good for a nice chat. He looked exactly the way the Germans must have imagined the ideal of the Nordic man, the only difference being that he had dark skin and black, wavy hair. He was always able to come by some pomade.

I saw him on board the train before it was sealed; he was shaggy but standing tall, capable not only of leading an athletic team but also of setting fire to all of Berlin, from where he came. His hair was even wavier than usual, because he'd run out of pomade.

For a great many people, life is like walking on a tightrope stretched over an abyss. One person walks over it—with or without a pole in his hands—almost smiling; another, clenching his teeth. A third may even fall with a smile. Or at the very least, fall without crying.

Such, I would say, was the case with Freddy Hirsch at that particular moment. He had probably told himself that he wouldn't give the Germans the pleasure of seeing him, with his beautiful body and fine face, look like a wreck. It's probably the same as when the boys in Number Sixteen play cards, and nobody for the life of him, not even if he were to lose his bread and soup ration for three days in a row, would dare to be seen moving a muscle in his face.

I realized that since Freddy Hirsch is from Germany, he may have been ashamed, and not on his account alone. He said that when he returned, he'd want to live in Prague—no longer in Germany.

Once, Mr. L. spoke about how we all are perfecting the art that no one wants to talk about, the art of dying, even as we each try to steal a bit of time from death. The art of losing probably came right after that on Mr. L.'s scale.

It has occurred to me how I had missed the opportunity to ask Mr. L. about the chances of doing something for Lida when I found out that she was to be included on a transport east. Ludmila went away as an adult, thanks to Harychek Geduld and thanks also to how we spent the last night before her departure on November 22, 1943, in Harychek Geduld's large room at L 218.

December 1. Once. A sixteenth of a loaf of rye bread. Five times. Ten marks. A children's abacus. A man's winter coat made of burlaplike material. Two grams of rice. Seven marks.

December 2. Once. A slice of bread with margarine and sugar on top.

December 3. Twice. A pair of men's leather gloves. One ski pole.

December 4. My earliest recollection in life is fading. I see a black and gray picture on the wall where my first crib was standing. I slept side by side with my brother and sister. The wall had just one window. The window did not look out onto the street, but rather into our living room, which had two windows facing the street. The name of the street was Kings Boulevard, and I remember that I used to be proud of that name.

I can't picture the whole wall, but I do see our living room. Only rarely do I see my bed, my sister or my brother or myself in my recollection. I manage to see just what was visible from the window in the wall through to the windows out onto the street and what was in between and then again what you could see right across the street, more windows, with everything else beyond beginning to fade.

Maybe that's why windows and lights are so important in my life—I don't know. It must be why I dislike dark rooms, black or dark furnishings, heavy or thick curtains, blinds for air raids or tightly shut doors, shut so tightly that you can't open them quickly or easily enough.

Though it's possible that I look at it that way only now, with the arrival of the first rumors about rooms without windows, and it doesn't matter that they used to be gymnasiums, riding halls, warehouses, or real bathrooms with real showers. I regard all steambaths with suspicion, and I have no desire to speculate too terribly much about all the possible implications of airtight doors, which have no doorknobs on the inside. I am equally suspicious of factory hallways and of riding halls.

Then I can see myself traveling as far back as I can go: an eight-branched candelabrum, brought into our household by Mama with her trousseau, a gift from her mother, going who knows how many grandmothers back. The candelabrum was either lit or had the white, slender candles ready. I don't know.

The mood in which I return to this memory, or what I have been thinking about or doing just before it comes, and also what awaits me after, most likely determines whether I see the candles lit or burnt out. I can see both, whichever I wish, but it is a blurred recollection in either case.

Of course, it's quite possible that I remember this only secondhand, from things people have told me since—my mother, father, sister, or brother. But now I really remember it. I am glad that one of the first things I saw in my life was the candelabrum, which Papa sometimes threatened to sell when it hadn't been polished for some time; but of course, he never sold it, since Mama never wasted any time proclaiming that he would do that over her dead body. It has become blurred with echoes of old glory and excitement, and ever since that time, I have liked candles of all sorts.

I suppose that ever since that time, I have been fond of celebrations, of music, and especially of brightly illuminated rooms and streets.

Looking back, I can see the candelabrum and the candles only through a wall. It was probably the first candelabrum and the first flame my mind ever noticed.

The candles would remain idle in the candelabrum for most of the year, until Mama came and lit them one after another over the course of several nights. Papa considered the legend that went with this to be an old and therefore innocent superstition, easy to live with. I would be in bed by the time they were lit, so that the remnants of the lighted candles were the first things I saw on opening my eyes in the morning.

I'm never really sure that things happened exactly the way I've written them here, but I do know that the reason the first experiences we have in life are so important, whatever they may be, is because we understand that they will stay with us till the end. And also, I'm beginning to imagine that all of the important questions in my life, like this one, will have to remain unanswered.

But when I look at it from a more positive perspective, I see the candelabrum and the candles as an echo of those old legends that reminded Mama of the one successful revolt, long ago, which blotted out all the unsuccessful ones, and the purification of what Mama knew by the word "desecration." I can hear, if only remotely, the echo of that victory that wasn't lost even in all the subsequent defeats, and there were so many of them. Mama knew the names of the kings, and she attempted to uncover some new meaning in each of their names.

I could never conceive of the labyrinth of old events and people and of what had preceded them other than as the echo of what came afterward and what perhaps goes on still. And so, by way of the eight-branched candelabrum and the candles, I can envision the window in the wall, a part of the wall, and a window out onto the street, which gave me a view of what was happening at the other end of the apartment and even across the street.

And while I am describing it, the image of that wall and of the window in it becomes more distinct. I'm glad, because I can see now that there was a door next to the window, leading into the bedroom and the bedroom leading into the living room.

The door was painted an enamel-like white and had a frosted-glass pane in the upper half, with some floral designs etched into it.

The frosted glass suddenly reminds me of wintertime, though not the skating and sledding that my brother, sister, and I had known but rather the winter here that is fast approaching. Should my writing include this? I'm relying on memories from a lot of different sources now.

But suddenly I feel I'll burst out laughing, for two reasons. First, what I'm writing is funny and insignificant, yet second, it is for me the only proof of my existence. And I can't even let myself describe what comes next because, third, I don't want it to run amok. And finally, there's something I'll call a fourth here. And that is, do I really remember the room and the eight-branched candelabrum with the candles, and the legends about the fearlessness and the bravery of all those unknown people invoked by Mama, or is it merely my recollection of old photographs, taken by Papa when I was little? I'll probably never find out.

At the same time, this memory sits inside me day after day, year after year, ever more firmly, exuding a pleasant, familiar, yet bygone aroma, like all memories. It's like when Mama used to bake pastry in the winter; the aroma lingers on inside me like a shadow attached to everything, even if I don't notice it at night or at noon, and even if it makes no difference where I picked it up.

December 5. Once. A glass of baby formula. Seven times. A big steamer trunk. A fur collar. Fifty-two marks. Two sets of bed linen. A box of ladies' handkerchiefs. A Parker fountain pen, gold. Twelve marks and fifty pfennigs.

December 6. When I told little Rabbi B. that I liked prostitutes, just as Mr. L. had liked them and Laszlo Berkovich likes them, I saw not only agreement but also something else written on his face. He was surprised that a steamer trunk served as my table and a wine bottle as my vase.

It is definitely much more fun to be with prostitutes than with a candelabrum, candles, flames, or a hole in the wall. For one thing, they are alive; they talk and give answers when asked something. For another, they are mostly good-looking, brazen, dressed in a funny way; and still another, they are the only ones I know who have real contempt for everything represented by objects and money, even if they know the value of those objects and of money.

I used to come across such women when I was still a little girl. I think I told the little rabbi that I don't include among such people the mother who needs aspirin for her child and doesn't know how else to get it. Or wives whose husbands need something right then and there or they'll face the danger not only of not being men but of not being, period. And I'm also not talking about the daughters who are trying to get their father, mother, sister, or brother off a transport without a Mr. L. at hand, as I have, and without knowing some prominent person, an officer or someone like that, not to mention people who are trying to get themselves off a transport.

I once had a friend named Pavla who lived in the house where I was born, in one of the oldest parts of Prague. The house was a five-story tenement overgrown with moss; in retrospect it reminds me of an old tree. Pavla was fat, ugly, and obnoxious. She had curly hair but was neither Jewish nor a gypsy. I didn't really care for her, but I used to play with her because she lived in the neighboring apartment, just across the hall, and because we were the same age and were in the same class in school. But the person I was almost madly in love with was her mother.

My recollection of Pavla and her mother is perhaps my second strongest recollection. In her mother's eyes there was a glimmer of something I can't even describe. It's found in only a very few women, just as, let's say, you can see it in just a few stars. In retrospect, I realize that even the most beautiful women may lack it. When they are cast out of their surroundings, as has happened to so many women here, they look even more depressed and decrepit than they really are.

I don't know how to describe this sparkle, but I do know that it exists. There is something in it that's independent and beautiful, as in some animals.

Pavla's mother was strong, calm, and level-headed. I never saw her flustered because of anyone or anything. She had the ability to wait and judge things for herself, though she knew how to get good and angry and to refuse to do something she didn't want to do.

She was full of energy, as if she were carrying an invisible flame inside herself, giving off warmth only to those people who knew how to handle it without getting burned. Nobody was perfect in her view, except for people who made the obituary notices. What I liked about her was her ability to see the future ahead of time, without worrying about whether she would be around to enjoy it.

I always had the impression when I was near her that she was capable of accomplishing more than she had, but that she was well aware of this and was in no particular hurry. She had expressive, beautiful features, for which people liked her, and something reliable in her eyes, which is why people confided in her. You can see a lot in a man's face, which represents him to the world, the way a visiting card does when given out to clients by a traveling salesman. She had a long neck, like an elegant horse, with her hair combed back into a braid. She wore lots of exotic makeup. Perfumed smells, chamomile probably among them, exuded from her even from six meters away. I remember her dark eyes and rich red lips. She usually wore a sweater, as tight as possible, so that her breasts stood out in a manner that was very womanly.

Most of the sweaters she bought had a V neck. She rolled her sleeves up to her elbows, and she had dark, very smooth skin. Sometimes she would get no sleep at night, or would sleep just an hour, or so Pavla would tell me. But she never looked tired.

Each time I see her in my mind's eye, I see her standing in their apartment. I don't think she had a husband. To get to the bathroom from each apartment, you had to go through the hallway, so that I used to see her in all kinds of outfits, from bathrobes to various housecoats, dressing gowns, and underwear, to elegant dresses, usually worn to balls, or in a fur coat, made of rabbit, under which, I bet, she wore not so much as a petticoat.

Later, Papa told me that she was not entirely without steady employment, as it appeared; she played in a women's band, though he didn't exactly know what instrument. Her apartment was more tastefully furnished than ours. Our apartment served its purpose well enough, but Pavla's mother's apartment had something else to it. There was about everything a patina of past, present, or future adventures. Their apartment was hiding a secret, the same secret that is hidden within some people's lives. I remember that you could sit, stand, or do whatever you wanted in Pavla's apartment. At our place, Mama with her "Don't do this or don't do that!" was always nearby. Pavla's mother couldn't care less what we did in her house.

I remember that she would often kiss very young men. I don't remember a single one of them in detail—rather, I remember the expressions on their faces. Or the way they gazed at her, as if they wanted something more than what they had already gotten, or as if they had missed something. The men really were remarkably young. As they left, some of them would yell unflattering remarks, which Pavla's mother would ignore.

On the way to the bathroom, I would sometimes see her having a fight with her young men, or sometimes I'd see her lying in bed with others, as if the world outside didn't exist.

Once, I ran into her in the hallway. She was barefoot, wearing only a long jacket with nothing on underneath, and she was laughing at the lad who, walking down the other end of the hallway, was yelling obscenities at her.

Sometimes Pavla's mother would stand in front of the mirror for hours on end, as if searching for something in her reflection that no one had ever found. She looked like an actress, with a beautiful face, beautiful breasts and hips, and elegantly slender legs. I really liked her. I asked myself secretly why my mother wasn't as beautiful.

Later, when I was older, she had a female visitor, perhaps her mother or grandmother, who told her, "You're a fool to care, a fool to give. Smart people know better than to give—smart people take." Pavla's mother gave the old woman a handful of money and laughed. The old woman took the money and left. Another time a girl visited her, perhaps about fifteen, with a violin in a black case. I overheard the words she said to the girl:

"Women who give for free, without asking anything in return, usually get nothing in return, whereas women who withhold their favors get rewarded, persuaded, and treated well by men. But men who only reward bitchy behavior constantly complain that women are bitches."

There were days when her hair changed color all at once and became red, while her red sweater became black and even tighter than usual. Her eyebrows were transformed, their arch remolded or trimmed down. Her eyes were as black and glinting as a flame. But that was no diabolic flame. There was nothing evil in it at all.

And in those days, beginning when I was four years old, I wished that I would look and act like Pavla's mother when I grew up.

Now and then, Papa told me later, I would run away from home. Mama would always hold me tightly by the hand during our walks, but I managed to break loose and run somewhere where I could discover something new. I remember how Mama used to worry about me.

Once, Mama told me how she had taken me to the river when I was two years old. It was the first time I had seen a river. We were underneath a long bridge, Mama holding me by one hand, an aunt by the other. They worried that I might be frightened of the water. I ran off, heading straight for the river. I was laughing and got myself completely drenched.

We moved twice. I had my own bed by the time we moved to our second house. I had a blue pillow, and my sister, a yellow one. After our parents turned off the lights, I would ask my sister what story she wanted me to tell her.

And when she asked what there was to choose from, I answered that I would take a look and tell her right away.

I would reach under my pillow and take out a golden key. No one was supposed to know about this. The chest to which the gold key belonged was tiny. It had two shelves. Books of all sizes were inside. But none of them had been printed yet. Only after I rubbed the tips of my fingers over their bindings did their titles appear.

I could talk for hours. My sister was fond of horses and was happy when she could mount one with her darling, riding off into a castle after dark, where she would get married every single night; whereas I would go off with my sweetheart for an entirely different reason. I preferred occasional meetings. I began to believe that I was as beautiful as people had so often told me I was.

I was convinced that when I learned how to read and write, I'd write stories that would give me pleasure. It seemed just as simple as going to sleep in a clean bed with the knowledge that on waking up in the morning, I'd see Mama as soon as I opened my eyes.

When I was fourteen years old, my life changed. Not only concrete things, but old dreams also, faded away. Matters that were always so clear-cut became suddenly vague, and I was gradually becoming less and less certain about anything.

I became aware of what might happen, like a person who knows when she goes to sleep and wakes up in the morning that her mother, who had always been there, is there no more.

That was when I knew that I no longer wanted to be a child. I wanted to grow up as fast as possible. It reminds me of how Mr. L. begged me, just before he went away, to stay with him just as he would stay with me; when I obliged him, he fell asleep just like a baby, just as when I was little I managed to sit for hours on the potty, till I fell asleep with a pacifier in my mouth. In the morning he said that it was as sweet a way for him to fall asleep as he had ever known. And that he wished that when his time was up, he would die just that way. Shivers ran up and down my spine, and it occurred to me just how strange it was that eventually everything came down to that. I can hear the melody of all the words I am writing down, trying to make them sound as true to life as when it all happened.

Once. A box of snaps.

When I am writing, I feel a flame inside me, and it occurs to me that I myself am that flame. I seem to be literally burning. It's not something I really know how to describe. There's something in it as strong as life itself.

From the moment I started to write my diary, I was no longer content with things just "happening." Only after I write them down does it seem to me that I have subdued the flame inside me. Yet the sensation of the flame and of burning is not connected with any particular thing around me. I don't know whether it comes from an unknown source and whether the greatest secret is truly invaluable. As if the words and the paper were telling me, "We will burn you up, everything, everywhere. With all your feelings and demands. But don't worry, if you persevere you may find what you are looking for." And the echo of those words seems to say, "Whatever you do." And I realize that what I have written can be only my truth. It too is like the wind or a wave, rolling in and sweeping me away, along with what I am standing on and what I am gazing at, lifting me up and carrying me off to some other place, where, without my knowing why, everything looks familiar; as if I had known it since time immemorial, always wanting to get there somehow, yet never having gotten there before.

I now know that I wrote what I wrote because I wanted to gain a sense of what has happened in my life and of what was important, though I never really managed to discover the meaning of it all.

From midnight on, I'm hungry. From dawn, I read the menu from last week.

MITTAG
MONTAG: *Fleischrisotto, Kaffee*
DIENSTAG: *Knödel m. Tunke, Kaffee*
MITTWOCH: *Nudeleintopf m. Fleisch, Kaffee*
DONNERSTAG: *Kartoffelsuppe, Buchte/Kreme*
FREITAG: *Kartoffel m. Tunke, Kaffee*
SAMSTAG: *Karbonadel m. Knödel u. Tunke, Kaffee*
SONNTAG: *Buchte m. Kreme, Kaffee*

December 7. Once. A camera case. Twice. An army knapsack. Twenty-five marks. Three times. A box of matches. A candle. A bar of soap. Five times. A quarter of a loaf of German army bread. A tomato. Fifty ghetto crowns. A kilo of potatoes. Six marks. I am almost afraid to be alone.

On my thirteenth birthday, I woke up in the morning, understanding all at once what just the day before had still been a secret. It seemed to me for the first time in my life that I was closer to death. That life was something fragile, like an egg in its shell, flying through space, where each speck of stardust could shatter it in a hundredth of a second. I felt meeker. Nothing was happening. It was a sunny morning. Silence hung in the air. All the people I knew were still alive. It is difficult to express it in words. Was it a fear of growing up and at the same time a desire to grow up? It was sadness and joy together. I didn't understand it. It became blurred with the feeling of inner emptiness. It arrived during the night. I woke up with the feeling or with its echo, or perhaps with its cause. That's how man wakes up one day, losing his innocence without lifting a finger. He is afraid of the new day, of feeling empty. Why? Probably no one knows why. And I knew that I could trust no one fully, as I could have only the day before, perhaps not even myself, and that I belonged to no one, and only partially even to myself. And then, various experiences began to confirm it—mine, my parents', my friends', everybody's. It would be difficult to say just how many times since that day I have awakened earlier than I meant to, with the fear of inner emptiness.

December 8. Once. A deck of cards.

Twice. A year-old calendar. A wine bottle with a candle.

Three times. A luggage lock and a name tag. Fifty marks. Twenty marks.

There was another dream I used to have, one that literally grew up alongside me. I used to dream it every night, sometimes several times during a single night.

When I was little, about four or five years old, Mama became ill. She was bedridden for more than six months with a spinal disorder. I was not allowed to climb into her bed, and Mama could not pick me up and cuddle me, as she had done before. I had become accustomed to going to her bedroom ever since I was a very little girl, but now I was frightened, seeing her lying there helplessly, her eyes fixed on the ceiling. I had no idea that she was sad and in pain.

She went away one day, and Grandmama began to take care of us. She cooked, did the laundry, and baked, staying with us in our house. Papa also hired a maid named Lisa to help Grandmama. They both bathed me and took me for walks, the way Mama and an aunt had done before. We needed Lisa because Grandmama and Papa used to go to visit Mama in the hospital, sometimes staying there for a long time.

The room in the dream was always empty, without any furniture except for a bed with a chair next to it. A woman was sitting on the chair, like a shadow; a man was standing next to her, in the middle of the room. Somebody was lying on the bed, and I was always afraid to come close. I snuggled up to the woman in the chair, crying and not daring to take even one step closer. The woman in the chair and the man standing in the middle of the room were trying to convince me that I shouldn't be afraid to move closer and say a few words to the woman lying under the quilt.

Now, of course, I understand that the woman in the bed was my Mama, the woman in the chair my Grandmama Hana, and the slim, scrawny-looking, strict gentleman was Mama's doctor.

I realized that the fear I felt in the dream was nourished by an incomprehensible loss that I could only begin to sense at that time and by the loneliness in which I subsequently found myself and that no one, including myself, has been able to explain to me ever since. The fear reflected my distrust of everyone around me, especially Papa.

The woman in the bed did not look even remotely like Mama. She was thin and very quiet. Her hair was long, braided at the back into a chignon and suddenly seeming scanty in its grayness. I know now of course that this was caused by the medicine and the various painkillers she was taking. She lay in her bed, weeping and calling out my name. But I was afraid to come closer, even though Grandmama Hana chided me and prodded me into doing it. In the end, she took my hand and led me to Mama's bed, saying, "Perla, this is your mama. Give her a kiss. She loves you. Can't you see that this is your Mama and that she loves you very much?"

I was afraid this was a trick, and I was not going to be taken in, so I would not for the life of me take a single step. Yet, in my mind, I fairly leaped up, bending over her to let her kiss me. Then I took Grandmama Hana's hand, asking her to take me out of the room.

I realize now that for a long time I wasn't sure about the identity of the unknown woman in the bed, though I knew all along that it was Mama's bedroom. The result was that I was afraid to be near anyone. I felt that nobody could be trusted. And that all my thoughts and desires had to remain my secret.

It seems strange to me that all of a sudden I am mentioning the story of my mother, of her illness and my dream. I have never told anyone. Everything else has come loose from inside me a long time ago, but this I am bringing up for the first time, even though it's only here, on paper. It seems that I didn't ever have anyone to share it with who wouldn't laugh at it or betray me.

It would probably sound ridiculous if I were to say that this paper is like my Grandmama Hana, or like Lisa, who took care of me all that time, or like a hole in the soul that can be filled only by my telling it to someone.

At the same time, it seems to me entirely proper for a seventeen-year-old girl like me to do this. It's almost as if that's all that she really needs to do. Even if her name weren't Perla but Dita. Or Jana. Or Margaret. Or whatever.

I have caught Lida's sickness. I keep asking why so many strong, handsome men can't just rise up against Hitler and his soldiers and deputies, against the Nazis here, against everything that is so infinitely sickening, minute by minute, day by day, year by year.

Mr. L. said, "Can you imagine what the fights of the gladiators must have looked like in the old days, with the Roman emperor watching a huge arena in which a man was pitted against a lion released from a cage in the wall? We know, if only from the mere echo of the fight as it reaches us today, what went on and the only possible way it could have ended. The point was not who would win or lose, the man or the lion. The point was whether the man would lose with dignity, in the lion's claws and jaws, or lose like some poor wretch. That's our dilemma as well. Mine and yours too."

"Men should fight," I said. "Women should fight too. Children also. I don't want others to say that we behaved like old hags."

"Do you think the Russians, the French, or the Americans would do any better in our place, left alone to face the lion in the arena, hungry, lonely, disdained by everybody, absolutely everybody, my dear, uncomfortable to all, before and after, to future victors as well as to future losers? Do you think they'd be so much as a hair, a fraction, a shadow different from or better than we are?"

"All the same, I think it's important to fight; men should fight, as well as women and children, all able-bodied people, cripples, old men, whoever has two hands and ten fingers or only one hand and five fingers with sharp nails," I repeated.

On the transport from the west there has arrived a Dutch pilot who is missing one leg and a forearm, having lost them when he was shot down in an English plane over Germany and on whose papers and between whose legs it was discovered just where he belongs. He has blue eyes and blond hair, and he walks on the promenade using two crutches. I think there is no other man in the ghetto who is more desirable to all the girls and women than our Dutchman.

Nobody asks him for details; it is enough for us to know that he used to be a flier, dropping bombs on the Nazis, to know that he was shot down with his aircraft and is missing one leg and an arm. I think that Mr. L. would be jealous of him. I think that all the men I discussed with Mr. L. are jealous of him. It is jealousy mixed with envy and admiration.

I hope the Dutch-English pilot will make up for what he is deprived of by not having one leg and an arm.

I would be happy if he knocked on my door, apologizing for coming without telling me beforehand, and so would many, many other Theresienstadt women.

December 9. I am becoming more and more pleased when I can light a candle or an oil lamp and sit down to do some writing. Once, in a discussion, Mr. L. conceded that the nature of writing encompasses something for which no substitute has yet been found and apparently never will be. But it is not only what you write but also when you write it. I can sense exactly when my voice is "authentic." I can't tell what it consists of, but I can tell when it is that way. I can feel it.

The old rat under the floorboards was really impudent today and noisier than usual. I heard that when a lot of rats come together, they throw themselves at people and are capable of eating them alive.

When I was little, it seemed to me that Papa had changed. He stopped talking to us, even though he went on speaking to us, just as before. As a very little girl, I used to be happy, and one of the reasons must have been my closeness to Papa. Although I later had almost exactly those same feelings toward Mama, it wasn't that way right from the start; much of what Mama did or said irritated me. Papa seemed to be more cheerful, carefree, and pleasant.

When I was ten years old, things changed. Papa no longer argued so much with Mama but now began to spend much of his time away from home, no longer paying as much attention to us as before. He hardly asked us about anything. And when he did ask, he didn't even bother to wait for an answer.

Who knows what difficulties he was going through? But for me it was as if lightning had struck out of a clear blue sky. It seemed to me that Papa had stopped noticing me, as if I didn't even exist. Mama's reaction to this was to distance herself instantly, or to at least turn her back on Papa. And I began chasing after Papa's attention in my own way.

With the passage of time, old suspicions inside me have grown stronger, even though the older they are, the less significant they seem to be. Did Papa know about it? Did Mama know about it?

I thought about Papa in a variety of ways. Some quite strong. Maybe I was obsessed with certain aspects of life, with no great desire to notice the others. Though maybe what I am speaking about must have terrified Papa at the time, not to mention Mama. Mama probably didn't have it easy with me. We fought a lot. She also began to look different in those days, though the result of it was that I began to like her better, not least because she no longer yelled at me so much.

I missed the times when Papa used to play with me, just as he had with my brother or my sister. It meant that he at least took some notice of me. And so I was left with Mama, though Papa was still around and his trips from home grew less frequent. I felt like a ghost around Papa. For me it was the worst thing in the world when someone acted as if he didn't see me, as if I were transparent, not there.

It was a long time ago in every way, even beyond the time gone by. But everybody carries with him everything he's lived through; it stays with him for the rest of his life, wherever he goes.

Once. A sixteenth of a loaf of rye bread.

I remember something that, in those days at least, I regarded as a misfortune. My favorite aunt, Elishka, had a stroke. Two days after she was taken to the hospital, my Uncle Albert had a stroke. They had no children.

They were both going on seventy and they loved each other. Then my brother went to the hospital with appendicitis, my sister, Rosalie, was bitten by a dog, and Mama found some earrings in Papa's pockets.

Why is it that the past seems so important or why, at any rate, does it stand out so much? Ludmila once said, "You aren't talking? Have you lost your tongue?"

"I have nothing to say," I replied.

"How can a man despise women when without women he wouldn't be, if you know what I mean?"

"I know what you mean," I said. "A great many people pretend that something that is the very condition of life is less important than the air we breathe."

"The longer we are here, the humbler we probably are."

"It's almost funny that a man is the precondition for a woman and a woman is the precondition for a man," I added, surprised at the way it sounded.

"Do you think that love or what goes by that name is courage, hunger, and fear?" I asked Lida all of a sudden. "Maybe it's also desire, hate, and contempt. One boy at L 216 told me, 'I have nothing at all against girls who feel freer than the wind, kissing and sleeping with whomever they want. They can take me right along; I would be a fool not to go with them. But I wouldn't want to marry such a girl.' "

Then, as usual, we went for a walk around the insane asylum. Courage, hunger, and fear? In the end, everything is included, I thought to myself. It's part and parcel of absolutely everything, including my old rat and even the reasons why we go for walks right here of all places. That's what people talk about the most, but also most of what is kept secret. Talk that appears to be virtually public property, as when the whole town buzzed about Diana and Reinisch, is really the biggest secret of all. People want it when they don't have it and don't want it when they have too much of it.

Before I learned how to follow my most secret desires, those half-suspected, vague longings and the longings of all other kinds, I felt lost.

"I once heard," said Lida, "that the female body has its own opinion and doesn't get pregnant until everything is ripe."

"I believe it," I said. "Besides, somehow it really seems to work that way. I often feel like I'm still a virgin. Virginity is something as nonphysical as it is physical. Old man O. once told me that when there's a long drought and famine in the desert, women lose their monthly regularity, so as not to bear children into the starving desert."

She hung on my every word, and behind her was the insane asylum overgrown with bushes; the insane had not yet come out, locked up behind barred and darkened windows.

"I've also reached the conclusion that men who like their mothers like women better than those who don't," I added.

"Why is that?"

"I don't know why. I can only guess from the way someone speaks about his mother how he might treat me. It has never failed yet. Men who like women, like their mothers."

"Do you think it's their way of paying something back?"

"I'd say they're continuing something," I said slowly, "as if the one embodied the other. Not to mention the fact that such men are capable of treating a woman far better. The woman too is better off with such a man."

We peered into the windows of the insane asylum. Some men dislike women. And vice versa. There's no explanation for it, or I'm not aware of any. But I do know it's true. Men need women just as much as women need men. Although it's only one kind of man who likes women because he understands them, admitting, without having to think about it, that women are capable of understanding him.

"Some men could like women, but don't know how," I added. "They know where the door is and they know where the keys are, but they don't understand that the lock needs to be opened at the right moment, unless they want to get in through a smashed-in door with a broken lock. I don't mean by this just the body, though much of it is the body. Sometimes one of them remains alive even if he's dead to such a perception. Either the man or the woman."

Still, something different goes on with some men, and you can't do anything but let go. Some men are like a room that is never anything but cold. For some, it's a room filled with the most pleasant warmth that they both take in and maintain. On the other hand, just as there are women like me who use their body as a weapon, there are men who exploit their manhood. As long as it's not a business, like when Lina Guggenheim's brother took his sister around, reminding me later of a wandering comedian going from village to village and from town to town with a trained monkey on a chain, collecting coins in a hat after each performance. Even though Guggenheim used to collect portions of powdered sugar, bread, or artificial honey, whatever people have had to pay with, just as they do with me.

This changes along with almost everything that

changes and almost before your very eyes. Only the insane asylum stands here and will stand here, even when the insane are dead and gone. At times, it's neither being a man nor a woman that's decisive, but a person's nature. People resemble animals, foxes, spiders, or beasts of prey; though I know that my viewpoint is almost too much mine, and that it doesn't apply to everybody.

Finally, I told Ludmila, "I think I'm glad to be a woman because women work much more simply than men. It's connected to so many things in boys that it's enough for just one thing to fail for their circuits to blow."

"What do you mean by that?"

"I'm not nearly as nervous as the boys are or the men I see around me," I replied.

I keep thinking how I had asked old man O., just before he went away, whether it would please him if I would lie down in front of him just as his models had when he was still painting. I felt bad at times that his fingers were mutilated in such a way that he was never going to be able to hold a brush in his hand, and I imagined how he would make a portrait of me and how I would stand in some beautiful house or even in a gallery, naked and white, with an expression that said not just what could be seen but also what only the best of painters would have seen, as if their gaze could reach deep or high.

He replied that I would be cold. I said that I didn't mind. I could easily put a blanket over me, just as I was, if he wanted me to. But I didn't want him to burst into tears at that moment, so I did it even before he said anything, staying there, lying next to him, for him to behold.

* * *

In about an hour we had had enough of a stroll, and Lida walked me back to my barracks.

I'm writing, staring at the pencil in my hand, the paper, and my fingers. Once, Mr. L. spoke about how trees grow; no one ever sees them grow and yet all at once they're tall. We all know that it isn't all at once. It only seems that way.

It has occurred to me that when I write dates, it arouses something inside me that I don't quite understand. Who knows what will still be of interest to people in the year 1999? My life seems like the air held in a child's colorful balloon. Is writing an attempt to catch the air that fades away against the sky or the water that flows between your fingers, an explanation of the inexplicable?

I changed the candle. I told several people to try to bring me some candles next time they come. Everything is the way it was before but, at the same time, everything has changed. Before Mr. L. went away, he brought me a whole box of candles. Some people recognize what's important even if the day before it wasn't important yet. At times, it's enough for me just to stare at the tiny flame. I only begin to write when words begin to sound the way they sound, when writing goes easily and when I know that it makes sense, if just to me. Often my writing contains different times: at the very least, the time that has already gone by and the time that is yet to come, the soul of people who have departed somewhere, or are no more.

The Cabalist introduced me to Rabbi B., whose wife had run away. I watched him watch me. Lately, I have been able to find some reflection of people who have gone away, including Mama, Papa, Mr. L., or Harychek Geduld, in the glances of other people. Sometimes I find it in unknown people whom I meet on L Street or Q Street. The worst is when I see Papa reflected even in the face of the Luftwaffe officer, who just paid me a visit again, almost surprised that I was still here.

"Such a little one and so much perseverance," he said, swallowing the word following the word 'little.' "

"We are allowed everything and we are allowed nothing," said the little rabbi.

He talked to me about a man who had heard his name spoken twice in a row by a voice in the sky and the wind. It seemed strange, but then, we all live divided between what was and what is. I, in turn, talked to him about Ludmila. He kept on about how the man had saddled up a white donkey, setting out with two servants, a stack of wood, a tinderbox, a sharp knife, and his youngest son, taking him along on the pretext that he needed his help.

He looked as if he too heard voices, echoes of the same voice heard by the man long ago, and as if it all had been turned around, with time moving backward rather than forward. He spoke about a fire on which the body of a boy instead of a lamb was to roast, as the proof not of cruelty but of the greatest of devotions. To me it sounded like some convulsive, topsy-turvy devotion. I wouldn't want to investigate how far it is from such devotions of the past to the disappointments of the future. Did that father gag his son so as not to hear his screams?

Rabbi B. didn't need to go on describing how the man kept glancing up and how, amid the silence of the hills and the desert, a conversation between a cripple and an invalid unfolded.

When I think of the prayers of the little rabbi, who even here won't eat anything that crawls and flies at the same time, or that contains worms or blood, I remember what somebody told me long ago—that there is no point in blaming a mouse hole for stolen grain.

But Rabbi B. wanted me to begin reciting along with him what had happened, without stopping at the moment when the old man, encouraged, confused, fortified, or possibly only frightened by his thoughts, placed the knife, sharp edge down, to cut his own child's throat and so spare him from being burned alive.

I thought to myself, that maybe had the father asked why back then, we wouldn't have to ask today.

I was afraid that he would want me to admit how much more merciful it was, because we all know, of course, that good things may become bad, but above all, that bad things can become still worse and those, in turn, the worst.

He wanted me to imagine the summons, the act, and the denouement. But he wanted me to leave out the invisible rain that put out the fire and to notice everything, the man, the hill, the son, and the fire on which he lay while his father kept averting his eyes.

He used fewer and fewer words, repeating the same words like "fire," "silence," and "heaven."

In the end, it always comes down to one choice: to sacrifice or not to sacrifice, to kill or not to kill. Why do we constantly try to convince ourselves that we have made great strides, as if that were so important? What's so good about having made such great strides? Wouldn't we have been better off going back to killing before they shipped us here like fattened animals earmarked for slaughter? Whom have we outrun?

"Are you trying to say that now it's Theresienstadt,

just as before it was Devil's Island, or Siberia, or the
stake of Torquemada?" I was hoping he wouldn't see
what this made me imagine in my mind.

"And before that, the Roman crosses, the Assyrian
spears, the Babylonian swords. In every generation
again and again, something is always found for us,"
Rabbi B. replied.

"Who needs to talk about it constantly?" I said. "I
hate people who use the first words out of their mouths
to talk about nothing but the suffering of the past two
thousand years, as if it still weren't enough."

Did he mean to say that what had been is and what
is has already been? All I can say is that, as the saying
goes, people are always closer to their shirt than to their
coat, but I'm not a rabbi, and he came with another
purpose in mind, not only talking about old times. He
asked whether I would have wanted it from my father?
I kissed his forehead. "What if my father had gotten it
from me?" I asked.

Then I said that I didn't understand why people say
it's better to have ten worries than to have just one. "We
probably don't like ourselves all that much," I said with
a smile.

He said that I had delicate, pure skin and that he was
thinking about how strange it was that each instant
seemed to be a mere chink through which everything
filters down to us. And I was glad that he didn't ask why
that man had not cut his own throat that day so long ago.

I waited for him to stop breathing so loudly, as if he
had just run in from the outside or was still running. His
eyes were red, as if he hadn't slept for several nights
before coming over here. Could it be that he had been
praying continuously before coming to me?

I waited patiently, glancing up occasionally at his

face, grown gray like the face of people who have been incarcerated for a long time. He was sweating. His eyes were teary, as if irritated by smoke. He kept rubbing them as if some ashes had flown into them.

I could see that he was far from being rested or relaxed. Then he spoke about a trial to which man would summon his one and only God. And with the evidence collected over a period beginning with the expulsion of our forefathers from Egypt, as if being born to our mothers was tantamount to having leprosy, through the Roman emperors, Spanish kings, caliphs, crusaders, and every conceivable rabble up to Adolf Hitler, he would condemn God to be a man.

I smiled because it crossed my mind to wonder if he might have come just for this. Would he send God to Theresienstadt? Theresienstadt, Post Office Bauschowitz, Langestrasse, No. 18, the way when Harychek Geduld used to receive food packages from his parents in Prague? I wondered whether he wouldn't be better off putting all those he had named on trial, but a quick glance at his red eyes was enough for me to leave him alone.

And so I was sitting next to the rabbi, thinking that I shouldn't disturb him, because the judge he had mentioned was none other than himself. Who would have said it about him, I thought. The rabbi was puny-looking, with a red scraggly beard and red hair, which he combed every other day at best. He kept gaping at me —and past me into the void—with his beautiful watery eyes that didn't tell me whether he was shedding tears, like the tears I shed when I peel an onion, or was weeping.

"All right, all right," I said vaguely.

And then I said, "I was always told that to be born

as a human being was the greatest privilege there was. Why make of it the harshest punishment?"

And finally, "What are you trying to prove?" I asked.

But the little rabbi didn't reply. He was probably suing God—had his hands full. He was most likely looking into the courtroom, or was it my attic with a rat under the floor, a skylight, and a straw mattress still quite decently stuffed, with no unpleasant smell of ammonia. My table, my chair, and my trunk, the beams, the floorboards. And the secret words, which only he heard, made up all the proscriptions of the law, three hundred sixty-five of them, exactly the same number as there are days in a year, as well as all the remaining laws, dispensations, of which there are exactly as many as the joints in a human body, six hundred thirteen in all, as the Cabalist informed me. He said nothing for quite a while. The trial was probably dragging on. God was pleading not to have to become a man; he's nearly human already. Nevertheless, he had to go on answering and confessing to the rabbi, as if it were possible through a simple decision to bring a conclusive end to anything, once and for all.

The evidence was complex and the little rabbi was probably taking care not to leave anything out.

My little rabbi looked stubborn, like someone who had been duped and deceived many times and, having gotten fed up with it, had finally reached his either–or.

But he looked as if he was frightened of his either–or, for he was now out of breath, with words stuck in his throat. He seemed to have discovered more incriminating evidence than he had expected.

From the way the little rabbi looked, as if he were choking with anger, crying from exhaustion, out of words and wanting to tell all with his eyes alone, his mouth half open, streaks of sweat spattered over him, his pants open at the waist, wearing a shirt in need of washing, it was doubtful that God could defend himself or that the little rabbi would drop the charges or at least put the trial off till the next day or indefinitely.

All at once, I felt as if my attic were in some tunnel between heaven and earth. I could imagine the court proceedings and all the depositions, examined from every angle, and the little rabbi maybe hearing his own voice, condemning God: "God, for everything you have permitted, I condemn you to become a man. As a man, you will receive a number and give up everything for which you have worked all your life, keeping only a hundred pounds worth of your worldly belongings, and you will report to the Trade Fair Palace, from which you will leave on a freight train to Theresienstadt, deprived of all the rights that separate man from beast, the inventor of fire, alphabet, and pride. But it will not end there. You will be hungry and you will be cold. You will lose your trust in the future. You will be ill, unable to find a doctor, and you will be alone, without the slightest idea of what has happened to those closest to you. And even if you find a place in some local lodging, you will tremble day and night with fears, spoken and unspoken, open and hidden, that this is not the last stop by any means, that next comes Buchenwald, Bergen Belsen, or Ausch-witz-Birkenau bei Neuberun, but you will no longer be able to invoke anything or anybody, disappointed as many times as you file an appeal because you will be one of us."

For an instant I imagined my old rat in the role of an associate justice. And the belts worn by German soldiers that read, "Gott mit uns."

In the end, judging by the way he looked, the little

rabbi must have gotten a glimpse of his God who was unable to file an appeal because he was a man and resembled Joseph Eisen from Block 12, Door 1-12, in the Sudeten Barracks, who had been given five weeks for taking two pairs of shoes, two pairs of socks, and an alarm clock from his roommate, and who had gone to unload coal onto a ramp on the night shift. Or he resembled Willy Falk, who had pulled ten weeks for six packages of food that he had expropriated from the post office. All defendants look alike in some way, I thought, while I watched the little rabbi, to see whether he was through with his trial.

I sighed. The little rabbi sighed also. I yawned. But now the little rabbi took another deep breath and from his eyes the tears came pouring out.

"Luckily, we have nice weather," I said. "They said we'd have a severe winter and that no one would get any coal or wood."

Then the little rabbi began to button up his pants and his shirt, put on his jacket, and wrap a scarf around his neck. Ashes were smeared all over his face, and as he was leaving, he looked hunched up, like a judge who had dropped something on the way over and now, on his way back, was looking for it, with his eyes cast down to the ground.

After he had left, I began to wonder whether he wasn't by chance weeping because he had had to set God free on account of insufficient evidence. Or for a surplus of evidence. Or because he needed to start again from somewhere.

When his wife left him the Cabalist later told me, he was left alone and I was the first person he visited. She was said to be just as tiny as Rabbi B. She was good-looking and used to spend almost eight hours a day standing in front of the mirror. She was obsessed with the glitter of mirrors. When she was with company and there was a mirror anywhere around, she would gaze over people's shoulders, looking at herself.

"How can you tell that the whole world is dying, when it may be just the two of us who are dying?" I said.

"By man's loss of respect for his fellow man," he replied.

There are times when I laugh because I am afraid, and now all of a sudden I was almost afraid of the little rabbi.

I went to look at the insane asylum. It was the first time I have gone alone. Everything appeared even more desolate and overgrown than before. Is Ludmila still worried above all else about going insane?

Deserted, the insane asylum looked even worse than when there were people in it. I was gazing at the bushes, at the leaves still left on the trees, as if seeking or expecting an echo of the words from my conversations with Ludmila.

Long must be the journey that every man has to take and that takes him through a tunnel, a thousand years long. It has occurred to me that each leaf that grows on the trees near the insane asylum can grow here only because there are those trees around. It's funny, but all of a sudden I feel like a leaf conscious of its tree. Fortunately, the gates of the insane asylum are locked, the windows blacked out from the inside, and the bars permit no one to get in, even if for some reason he wanted to.

I remember how Ludmila said unexpectedly it was a good thing that there are insane asylums.

* * *

Once, Ludmila and I talked about rats and I could see that it took all her strength to talk about rats the way you might talk about the weather. But she herself had started it.

"Do you keep a rat or an entire rat colony?"

"As it happens, I keep just one old queen rat," I said. "Once, another rat came over and I thought from the way they ogled each other that they would get together, but my rat all at once attacked the other one and chased it away."

"Is it true that only rats and people kill their own?"

"I say I don't know when I don't know, Lida," I replied. "What about wolves? And crocodiles?"

"Where there are people, there are rats," said Ludmila. "They're even aboard ships."

"You can turn it upside down," I suggested.

"I find it encouraging that people have not gotten rid of them, even though they've tried awfully hard, just like the Germans have with us. Therefore, any resemblance between us, even an accidental one, is comforting," she added.

"I don't know too much about rats; for instance, Mr. L. claimed that rats, like owls and snakes, are nocturnal animals, but my companion's tastes seem to go the other way. They breed like rabbits. Maybe rats understand human customs better than some people," I said. It bothered me that Lida was comparing herself to a rat.

"Only rats and people seem to be capable of surviving what can be survived," said Ludmila.

"Let's drop it, all right?" I asked quietly.

I felt sick to my stomach. But she too felt sick to her stomach, though it wasn't from the rats. Talking about rats, she was trying to hide something else. She wanted to tell me that rats, not we whose great-grandmothers and great-grandfathers had been blamed for it, had transmitted the plague in the Middle Ages—and are transmitting jaundice now. Someone told me that most rats live in harbors, in rivers, and at sea, probably because the biggest stores of provisions are there, granaries, the most important thing people have—food.

In the end, everything comes down to food. I'm pretty sure I still have a normal sweet tooth.

Lida and I received at that time a ticket to go to the café, and we kept running into people who were watching the Ghettoswingers. These folks were living or were able to live almost anywhere, as if in a dream.

The ticket was given to me by the manager, Mrs. Itsikson, who not only looked like Pavla's mother but had most likely practiced the same profession before working her way up.

I know that when the café opened, she used to tell the local waitresses, as if they were somewhere in London, "You may accept anything in the world, dear ladies. Gold, silver, jewels, or one mark and twenty pfennigs. But it's got to have class. As my mother used to say back in Ruthenia: 'If you have bread, you'll always find a knife to cut it with.' "

Mrs. Itsikson told us how she had started her career at a bar. And how she used to make fun of the guests at first. She lied to them and they lied to her. She gave herself various names: Martha Andreotti, Cecily Bernini, Rosalie Fergusson. Once, after work, she invited a sailor she really liked to come up to her room. At the end, he dropped fifty crowns from his pants pockets onto her bed. She told him he had dropped some money and asked him to take back the fifty crowns. He answered that she could keep it. She took it as a bad joke. But then she discovered that what appeared at first to be a game or a joke was gradually becoming unpleasant indeed, because it was becoming the truth. But when she told the truth to her guests, they thought she was lying anyway. In the end, she wasn't even able to convince them of her real name.

"The music here is nice," I said.

"If you can wait, you'll get to hear some that's nicer still," said the manager. "I'll see to it myself."

"I know," said Lida. "It will be like a poem by Harychek Geduld, how we'll arrange for reparations after the war, paying us back for each day we'll have wasted here."

"That's clear," I said. "A person will simply go to a cashier's window between ten and twelve in the morning and a gentleman in a black suit will pay out the appropriate amount to everybody for each day he'll have spent here."

"It's never too late, when you are a German," said Lida.

Mrs. Itsikson looked at me, smiled, and went her own way.

Once, in a calm moment before we started working, Mrs. Itsikson told me, "Somewhere between the ages of nineteen and twenty-two I discovered that my relationships with men were the most important thing in my life. I had this ability to find something appealing in almost all the men that I met. Old men, young boys, carpenters, waiters, priests, Spanish, German, Jew, or Arab—they all were men and I was fascinated. How does an attractive young woman, who has these feelings, hide her secret from the world and maybe from herself? She gets married. The secret that I carried so deep in my heart from the moment that I married until my first affair outside of marriage tortured me for years, and it was only the role of motherhood that eased the pain. Had I gotten married to run away from what I thought I might become? Why were men and my feelings for them and understanding of them so strong a force within me? Certainly this was an uncomfortable secret; it frightened me, and I wondered if I would ever understand why I married when I did. Years later, after having left my husband, I began to understand my own needs as a woman to feel the world around me, and that need included men in my life, who continued to bring me new and exciting feelings about myself as a woman."

Once. Some stationery, with the monogram V.W.

Somebody sent me the message that I'm dangerous, that my existence inconveniences him, and that I'm noisy at night, not to mention what an unpleasant sight I make out on the street. Now that Mr. L. is gone, I have obviously been occupying my garret for too long.

I am rereading what I have written. I know that my poor "writing voice" is the only thing that is really mine. I don't have to compare it with anything to know that even though I have moments when I want to shout "That's it!" my enthusiasm evaporates almost as quickly as it came. I would like to accomplish as much as I can in as short a time as possible, but I also see the clearest of pictures slipping through my fingers, like sand. I'm trying to get rid of inconsequential details. Once in a while my writing goes smoothly. By "smoothly" I mean that I know almost exactly what I am writing and I don't start sentences with excessive energy that whispers into my ear, "If you don't put this and this down instantly, you'll forget it; it will be lost and you'll never again retrieve its essence." And if I don't see my writing this way, I'd rather put down my pencil in every way, even in my mind.

I never understood it when people told me that it was somehow depraved, which is what they told the other girls. And that I shouldn't start something if I didn't want to lose something that everybody has only once. I doubt that you shouldn't start something unless you're about to marry the man. But perhaps, since people have made so many nice things ugly for themselves, this had to be included as well.

I think everyone has a limit, enabling him to open his arms to one person or to eighteen. This is what Ludmila and I did before Harychek Geduld and his team from L 218 departed, with Lida getting what she'd always wanted, eighteen-fold. Some people arrive at eighteen all at once, while others take their entire lives getting there.

Some people's lives are long, others' very short, that's all I have to say. I remember clearly the tension of my first brushes with sin. There is a kind of cement in it that both holds my life together and splits it into pieces. I could swear it's the truth. What I do can be the best of bonds, in which I seem to merge with people, the world, everything that life stands for, in some basic way. Even though it, like everything else, has other aspects as well. But first and foremost, such coming together is pleasant. It contains something without which I feel lost. But there is a thin line here, over which I mustn't step if I don't want to damage something that is still to come.

Second, when I see that someone is losing interest, I am at the same time losing something good that was in me until then. I think many people know it right from the start. And it's true, as I once told Harychek Geduld, that I can open up to almost everything, embrace the whole world. And third, it contains a key that enables me to recognize who is who and who I am with this or that person, and what the pluses and minuses are.

I think it's a kind of love that only mothers feel. In a mother's relationship with her child there is, on the mother's part, a sort of overall acceptance, revealed long before we are born and shown just as much in the mother's body as in her child's—as in mine.

There's no contract for it—which someone fulfills and someone breaks. It's not pride, even though pride is also a part of it. It encompasses carefreeness and devotion. A celebration, for which we need ourselves only, no riches, no castles, no estates or islands. Occasionally, when not enough time remains, it can be a celebration for all of us together. There are days when I feel blind and deaf and insensitive, all my faculties dead. And then there are other days. With me, it shows itself above all in that one place. I feel the world most strongly between my legs.

I have the feeling that I could really get to know the entire world with just that. And there's enough of it for, let's say, three hundred people all at once. And then there's something else as well. This all-embracing feeling doesn't last long. It ebbs, and afterward I no longer feel so nice.

There are times when I go back to the days when I first started to go out with boys. I couldn't believe that men could be afraid of girls to such a degree that in the end girls had to run after men. And the result was that each boy who showed the slightest interest in me when I was twelve or thirteen was for me something like what Friday was for Robinson Crusoe on that desert island.

It always had to do with knowing—this was the thing—
things that after a while acquired a life of their own. I
knew what I would expect of myself if I were a man even
if only for a short while.

I remember that Papa once sent me to stay with my
aunt in the country. It was during a hot spell, and I was
hoping every day that something would happen. Then I
discovered a barn at the end of the farm, just at the edge
of the forest, in a clearing where a huge lime tree was
growing and where the teacher necked with a woman
from the farm every night. They began by the tree, and
then, hiding under a cart, I could watch them make love
in the moonlight, under the stars. I envied the woman.
I wished I could be in her place. I wished that the
teacher would take turns with us and that I would lie
there, kissed and made love to by him, now and then.
I'm sure that when I later gazed at him and began to say
hello, the teacher must have been aware of my innermost
thoughts. He smiled back at my greeting, like someone
who was aware of a secret that bound us together.

I remember how much I hated coming back from
vacation, but before I finally left, the teacher gave me a
good-bye kiss right on the mouth. I have forgotten many
of my teachers. I have never forgotten that kiss, that
teacher.

It occurs to me now that he might well have known
that I had observed them kissing and making love. The
woman probably knew nothing, but he, in all likelihood,
was well aware of it. Could he have thought, like old man
O. on the day when he escorted Ludmila and me to
Fledermaus at the Fire House, that he was with two
women simultaneously, with a fully grown-up, ripe
woman and with a girl, actually a half child still? Why
do men want it?

He was a smiling redhead, dressed more like a laborer

than a teacher. He had strong arms, broad shoulders, and narrow hips, like the actor who played Tarzan when I was little, when Papa took me to the movies. I never stopped liking him and never stopped daydreaming that it was happening all over again and that over there, in the hay, in the moonlight, near the fragrant forest, on a hot summer night, he was making love to me and to that woman or to that woman and to me.

I recall an incident that occurred when I was probably no older than six or seven years old. It was after school and I believe that I had invited three or four boys from my class to come over to our apartment after school. I must have known that my mother wouldn't be home. I remember putting on her favorite robe. It was dark blue, with large bright flowers on quilted cotton, and it tied at the waist. I thought that I looked very grown up in that robe. I invited the boys, put on some music, and danced for them the most exotic dances that I could imagine. I felt a great sense of power as I watched their faces, which seemed to me to be completely intrigued with their mystery of me. After I finished dancing, I politely asked them to leave, and then I went to my bedroom, took off my robe, and looked at myself in the mirror for a long time and decided that I must be very special.

From that day on there was a secret that I felt about myself, not that I could have put it into words, but the sense of mystery and excitement that I felt was the first awareness of my femininity, and I have carried the secret of my brazen invitation and dancing for those little boys ever since.

By the age of eleven my body was developed and I had been experiencing the pleasures of being with myself. Most certainly, this was my deepest secret—to discover that my body and especially those parts least mentioned were able to bring so much pleasure to me. The most important part of the secret was not that I was doing something that I thought was forbidden but that I had discovered something wonderful about myself, that no one in the world would ever know because it was my very own body and I could bring about the pleasure alone, without need of anything else around me.

I kept the secret of my self-fascination for a long time.

But my first real experience goes back still farther. I remember how I would lie in bed with Papa and what it was like falling asleep next to him, curled up into a ball, feeling him next to me. It never occurred to me that Papa might have had some other thoughts.

Once.

I have only a faint recollection of the pain and the blood, which I'm almost sure was there.

At school I began to make friends in the early grades, though I always retreated the instant it seemed that a boy would accept my invitation. That was an echo of Mama, who was shocked at anything connected with boys, sex, or illness. And so, I preferred "friendly" relationships, with occasional touches and kisses.

But the underlying feeling was that of wanting to get it over with. My first real man was a nineteen-year-old plumber, who invited me into an apartment he had borrowed, where there were heavy curtains and a lamp that, as I remember, he turned off as I became nervous. The lamp cast a strange light on everything, and then the darkness was strange as well. I don't think he wasted any time. Something told me, "Now it will come, this is it." I remember that I wanted to take a good look at him. I wanted to check out the most important thing.

I began to think about Mama and about Papa. I was afraid that I really didn't know anything. I was perspiring all over. I might have looked as if I had been doing such things for a long time, but I was becoming more and more afraid. I remember that he became frightened. "What's the matter?" he asked. I replied that it was the first time that I had been with a boy in that way. Even though in a corner of my soul I was thinking that it wasn't so. He began to be just as nervous. "I had no idea," he repeated. "You were not at all afraid." He talked about my fear while covering up his own. And we were both nervous because there was not a single trace of this being the first time I was with a man. He turned on the lamp. He was probably scared of my being so young. And then it occurred to me that he could have simply asked, I would have answered, and everything would have been clear. Later I was able to explain it to myself; because it happened again. In reality, he did not want to become entangled in anything; he was only interested in my body, in the more pleasant aspect.

I felt miserable for the rest of the day. The night was awful. And the morning worst of all. I repeated to myself, "God, why did you allow me to sleep with that plumber?" But at the same time, I laughed almost hysterically. In reality I was happy that I had done what Mama had done before and my aunt, my grandmother, and all the women in my family who had ever been married. Only I spent the whole day in fear that Mama would see somehow. She saw nothing.

That was the first thing that taught me not to worry so much about tomorrow. Sometimes it worked out well, other times not so well. At times I was pleased and at others sorry. It's possible that in this respect people overestimate others because in most cases they underestimate them at the same time. I had always had the tendency to make my own rules in life. Though whenever I made some, I was the first to begin disliking them —maybe because they could never last for more than a day, a night, sometimes not even that long. But I knew there had to be "something," since there were people who wanted from me the same thing that I wanted from them. And I know that I have something that is mine, and yet not for me alone. I never believed that it could be only bad. Though it probably can't be only good, any more than everything else in this world.

I feel as if I'm sitting or walking on needles. I have a headache. It is again the unexpected change, even though nothing happened but that which makes everything that has to do with my life seem suspicious. Where does it come from? Where does it return? Where does it all lead? It seems to me now and then that what I need is a needle, quite a long one, so that I can pierce my head right through all the way to the brain and let some fresh air in. It's as if everything were covered up by anxiety from everything and nothing.

December 12. Three times. Twenty-three marks. A sixteenth of a loaf of rye bread. A bag of dried vegetables for soup.

I have diarrhea. At times I have diarrhea from the food; at other times, only because I don't know what is going to happen.

PART III

December 13. Once. A bar of chocolate. Three raw potatoes. Five marks.

December 14. Just before Ludmila's departure, as I walked her to the platform for her transport, carrying one of her boxes wrapped with rope, she asked me, "Do you believe in the devil?"

I glanced at her. "Do you?"

"I have the feeling that I have been and still am meeting him daily," she replied almost sadly. "And if you ask me whether he has horns, hooves, and bristles or whether he squalls like a monkey, I'll have to say no. He looks like a soldier in a uniform, like an office worker in a vest, with a watch that he never forgets to wind, or like an insurance agent. And it's not just men but women too. He talks to me at times but never tells me exactly

what's going on. You don't have to gape at me the way
you did at Melissa F."

"I know," I said. "And when he speaks, he speaks
German."

"Of course, he does speak German, though he speaks
in his own language."

"And does he always look like a man?"

"I don't think you'd believe me if I told you what he
looks like. You wouldn't even dream that that's what the
devil looks like. Sometimes he's the wind, the rain, a
snowstorm, or a freight train. At times he's a hope or an
illusion. But he's also the moment when buildings col-
lapse because he's an earthquake, or trains colliding, or
drunken soldiers flinging themselves at women on their
way from the Casino. Yesterday, for instance, he showed
me how I ought to hang the transport number on my
neck, saying, 'I never miss a thing, and you'll never get
another chance.' "

"Maybe he lied," I said.

"I'm glad that I'm going; everything looks degenerate
to me anyway."

"To me it only seems degenerate when you kill somebody who didn't do anything to you or you don't kill
somebody who, on the contrary, did so much to you that
he deserves to be killed for it," I said. Then I waited
with her for her train, so that we would know for sure
that the cars would be attached. As we all know, before
each transport they say that the Germans are out of
railway cars or that the tracks to the east are out of
commission, but so far the trains have always arrived
and departed on time.

"He's sometimes tinier than a pinhead," I said.

"You know, if it's the way they say it is, I'm going to
undress as the very last thing I do," said Ludmila.

"Who knows how much of what's said is the wildest of inventions," I replied slowly, so as not to make her suspicious. I was thinking about the clues that I had put together on the basis of what Mr. L. was able to tell me. I was thinking about my day and night dreams, about the Luftwaffe officer. "Hold my place for me there, but keep in mind what I like," I added.

"How do I look to you?"

"You mean, what do you look like?"

I was glad that Ludmila had grown up the night before in a way that was so important to her. She was going away in the same coat in which she had arrived and into which her father had had a thousand-crown bill sewn while they were still in Prague. She was wearing warm felt boots, good enough for Siberia, a scarf around her neck, and a blue beret on her head.

"You look fine," I said. Just the day before, Ludmila had kept asking her kind of questions, as if she were unable to comprehend what people could be made to swallow, and I don't mean just women. She really looked as if she were off to a center for winter sports, like some of the Jewish women who arrived now and then from Berlin. As far as they were concerned, babies could have been talked into their bellies.

"I hope you have really good underwear," I said again. It's strange that people who are about to go away look so beautiful. People whom we know we'll never see again.

We talked for a little while longer; I mentioned, as casually as I could, that I was afraid that the right train for me had left already and that when I go it won't be so plush in the boxcars. And Ludmila refrained from saying that in the end no one will miss a thing, so I needn't worry. She straightened the number on her neck, as if it were a pendant on a gold chain and not a piece of cardboard with the number 137 on a hemp string. She picked up her boxes. Then I sent my regards through her to all of my acquaintances she might run into in the east.

Once. A bouillon cube. A hair net. A bathrobe. Two marks.

I've come up with the idea of collecting in my mind the last words that everyone spoke just before leaving on a transport east. Mama: "You have such a small head." She said nothing else and it keeps ringing in my ears; why did she say that, of all things? My sister said: "It's raining." My brother asked: "Aren't you still sleepy?" Papa smiled: "We'll wait for each other." Harychek Geduld could be heard saying: "Each time fewer cars." Mr. L., I recall, stroked my hair, fixing his eyes on me, as if wanting to engrave me in his memory: "Only once. Everybody only once." And Laszlo Berkovich: "It's always merrier with kids." Milena: "I may tell you over there." The father of two little girls who had arranged for them to stay in Theresienstadt, going himself in the meantime: "Stay together." Why did Mama say: "You have such a small head"? Joseph Reinisch said to Diana: "It's all for the best this way." Somebody told a little child: "You've got to be strong."

But the conversations that preceded the transports were also strange, like someone going out into the rain without clothes on and making believe that it wasn't raining, something like that. Someone was saying, teasingly, "We are leaving but you've got to wait." A handsome gentleman might have whispered to himself, "Look up high." Ah, I said quietly to myself, "high," is that the same as "deep"? He was dressed as if he were off for a vacation in the mountains or by the sea. He must have had a beautiful life, I thought to myself. A mother told her child not to forget to tie his laces properly. Somebody asked how many cars the train had. And whether it was a transport for work. It was good that both men and women were going and that no old people were on the transport —it probably really was a work transport.

Once, Mr. L. told me that people, before touching the high-voltage wires, talk about such things as whether the weather looks like rain or, on the contrary, complain about hot spells in the summer. Some suicides, back in the time when they had the chance to prepare everything in peace and quiet, wrote farewell letters in which they made believe that they were setting off on some journey, leaving instructions to the bereaved as to where to find the key to the cellar, which bill needed to be paid next month, and other such things. Diana von Dubai answered Reinisch with the same words, and it was probably the last thing that they said to each other in this life: "It's all for the best."

And so, here I am with the last words of people who are here no more, and I can still sift through them.

The first secretary of the Council of Elders made an effort, before leaving, to stand up straight. Perhaps this was his way of making a statement. I had the impression that in the last words people spoke before their transports departed they discovered that things that had been important until then were not so important for those staying behind. And also that a lot of it was different from what people had said about it.

I don't know. I don't know. I don't know. I wondered what I would say if I were to leave now, but first I would have to think to whom I would say it.

* * *

Once. Some rat poison. A vial of aspirin.

The last time Mr. L. and I didn't manage to get anything done because I was ill. At times I get the flu and
it's nothing, and at other times it takes me three days
before I recover my senses. Mr. L. came to visit me
twice, covering me once with his shaggy fur coat, which
he was allowed to keep as a member of the Council of
Elders, while others had to turn theirs in to the Nazis.
Maybe he shouldn't have told me what he had told me
once before, because I kept imagining first Harychek
Geduld, then Ludmila, and finally myself in a barrel of
ice-cold water for twelve or sixteen hours and then that
somehow I was being measured. Or I saw myself as a
member of the scrub colony, using a whisk and a mop
to rinse red stains off the wall from which infants had
been bounced back and forth.
He brought me some aspirin, but I never swallowed
them. From the cellar I could hear the playing of the
crazy music teacher who had moved in here in the fall
and had kept playing his violin even in the bitterest cold,
so as not to get out of practice, or so he claimed. I didn't
wash for three days. Mr. L. stroked my hair. He was
pleased when I had a neatly combed part in the middle
or on one side. He said I reminded him of a girl by the
name of Eleonora Templeton. But this was a far cry from
the reasons he had been visiting me only a few weeks
ago, when he repeated how much he enjoyed gazing at
my head and face while I lay there, and gazing at himself
at the same time.

Mr. L. took my photograph with him to Birkenau. I
wrote on the back, "Not much to remember me by—
good luck in the future, love, Perla."

* * *

The night before his departure, Mr. L. dreamed about having a garland of oxeye daisies on his head. He heard some tunes that he had never heard before.

It doesn't help much to gaze at a straw mattress, which is what I've been doing for some time now. Though my mattress is certain to be better than those of ninety percent of the people here, it hasn't been refilled for a long time, and it contains a deep sag that could comfortably fit both me and my suitcase, if it came to that.

There is an old rat underneath the floor, who cannot but betray herself by scratching.

Milena, before she went east, told us, back at L 410, about some of the experiences of her religious upbringing in the Catholic school she'd gone to before the authorities turned up Jewish grandmothers on both her father's and mother's sides.

She was in that school until she was thirteen. In their needlework classes, the priest kept threatening them with the most horrible punishment if they ever allowed men to touch them before what was forbidden became sacred, and then rewarded their restraint. What a tantalizing terror this evoked in the girls, and how they touched themselves before daring to go further, how they ceased to be afraid of the street after dark, of darkness, and of corners in the park, and of dense bushes. No thick black bristles ever grew on their necks; they grew no horns and weren't smitten by any deadly punishment or anything remotely like it afterward. The terror gave birth to an anticipation that we all know only too well.

* * *

I told Mr. L. that I would divide loyalty along a clear line between two souls and two bodies. Incidentally, it was the young priest who later seduced Milena.

Once, Milena told us how she made her way into the local Catholic church at night and what she had discovered there. She said that a young priest used to come there through underground tunnels, built in the time of Maria Theresa. The Germans had not destroyed these catacombs and tunnels because anybody could see that they were ideal antiaircraft shelters and hideouts. Then Milena found out that there was a hidden mechanism in the altar that moved it aside, revealing stairs into the tombs and tunnels, leading to the cliffs and then to the Eger River. One night she saw the priest administer confession to a Jewish girl. She couldn't hear all the details because, as she said, the priest and the girl were whispering. Then they had to hurry up because morning and light were coming. As she told it to Ludmila and me, she kept smiling, as though she were hearing in her mind the Catholic priest discussing things with the Jewish girl that we would never find out about.

Only Ludmila asked her once why she had invented a Catholic priest and a Jewish girl, of all people. And then Milena and her secret left for the east.

As I see it, I like or dislike people for different reasons, at times giving a lot of thought to it all, to what man is made of. Maybe this has something to do with moods that I didn't yet have when I was fifteen. These are feelings that come up from the bottom of my brain by way of a secret path, a sadness for no reason or an inexplicable joy and then a headache. Mr. L. knew how to deal with it, but I know myself that I can live through it, if I can just last a couple of minutes, or hours. I never told him that of all the things about him, it was his voice I liked the best. I heard in it not just his fifty-one years but also something of his real self, who he was, including what he meant to me. Everybody reveals himself in some way, and as far as Mr. L. was concerned, it was his voice that reflected his truest self. Afterward, everything resembles sleep anyway. The moment when men fall asleep. And even when men look angelic because they look innocent. I don't know. It's like a river that comes and goes.

He was nervous at that time, perhaps also because he could see that now he wouldn't be able to take his coat back from me. He had the impression that his head was ticking, he said, with a thousand wound-up clockworks. I asked who wound them. Then he arranged for me to get coal rations, so that I could heat my garret.

Afterward I began to reflect on the different kinds of reality, beginning with the rats, who are as cold as I am and are scratching on the door, underneath the floor, and in the corners of the walls, where they have their holes, and extending up to the sky where the stars glow, even though, as Mr. L. pointed out, they have long been dead.

Maybe it's the same with people like ourselves, because a great many people resemble rats, not just in the way they look but also in what they do, and a great many of them, on the other hand, resemble the stars whose light is dead. Isn't the memory of people in fact something akin to the light of stars that long ago became extinct?

The same thought crossed my mind again when Lida was leaving, and I was gazing at the fifty boxcars, with a hundred people in each, watching them disappear around a bend, the entire train.

* * *

Ludmila didn't like Mr. L. Once, she told me, "I knew a man like him. He bit his wife's breast."

"Out of love or out of anger?"

"I don't know whether people like that are really passionate while making love, but I do know for a fact that they can become enraged to distraction."

"So why did he bite her if he loved her so much?"

"He was a poet," replied Ludmila.

"Do you mean to say that Mr. L. is likely to bite my breast one of these days?"

And to Ludmila's silence: "You are obsessed with biting. It isn't the first time you've spoken about someone biting somebody. Do you mean to say he bit off her nipple?"

"Do you think it's possible to bite off someone's breast?" Lida asked, almost quietly.

Twice. A writing pad. A frame for photographs. Five marks.

I found among my things a postcard that Harychek Geduld had received last April from his parents in Barmherzigern Gasse, Prague VIII:

> My dearest boy, I have received your kind card and am glad that you have gotten the shorts and the socks. Henry's address is: Birkenau bei Neuberun. Oberschlesien. You must indicate the year of his birth on your card. December 17, 1922. I wish you pleasant holidays. Take care and remember your loving parents. Best regards to Fritzie, Vera, and Fernie Weigert.

The canceled postage stamp showed Adolf Hitler, as usual, with his moustache.

December 15. Twice. A hard-boiled egg. Ten marks. Three times. Vaseline. Toothpaste. A bar of soap.

Who does old man O. speak to about Africa, lions, snakes, secret celebrations, and about a subterranean city at the edge of the Sahara? Once, he told me that at one time they had also been killing us off in the Balearic Islands.

Ludmila's worst fear had been that she would be sterilized in the east, or given injections that would change the makeup of her blood and her hair and eye color, after just such a rumor began to make the rounds here. I had asked her why it would bother her so much.

"I don't think I'm in any particular hurry to have children; nonetheless, there is certainly a difference between having it be up to me and having the decision made regardless of what I want or don't want."

And she said, as if two Ludmilas were talking inside her, "They are killing us off like flies. Like flies."

"They are trying to leave alive only the most beautiful people in the world," I said, hoping that Ludmila would understand my point. "The Nordic race, its skull, nose, eyes, everything. It's like an elimination contest. It's perfectly normal. What do you want? The most beautiful people will be allowed to make children but only with the purest bred, and it will all go as smoothly as sliding on ice, so that again, only the most beautiful children will be born. And should a child with a crooked nose, black hair, or squinted eyes be born for some reason, they will break his nose, pluck out his eyes, or tear out his hair along with his scalp, like the Indians. We will just stand and watch and be envious of them, ashamed to glance at ourselves; such beauty, such purity of blood, and everything according to the strictest prescription, lost to us, not possible even if they were to cut us up or rearrange us."

Ludmila was silent. Mr. L. had explained the racial theories to me, even though in practice we all know what they are really about. I was taken aback when I found out that not just the Germans but the French and the English also began to believe in them. Does it mean that if I were born German, French, or English, it would not be as clear-cut to me as to the person who is born of a Jewish mother? Would I think similarly if I were German and not Jewish? The Germans have given it the crowning touch, Mr. L. concluded. And it can't be blamed only on the fact that Hitler had to spend his nights in all kinds of flophouses in Vienna when he was a youth or that he'd never learned to paint, the way old man O. did, and is taking his anger out on us now. German soil, German blood, purity of race. So we aren't allowed, Ludmila, Harychek Geduld, Ernie H., and I, to plant seeds on German soil. Fine. We are unable to prove that we haven't had, for at least four generations, Jewish or colored ancestors. Is everybody with a pedigree Teutonic? Would Rabbi B., if he had been born an Aryan, be beautiful, majestic, and restrained? Does being Jewish mean being demonic, sensuous, and extravagant? Is the mixing of races so beastly? According to Hitler, Mr. L. says, there are three kinds of people: the founders of civilization, the guardians of civilization, and the destroyers of civilization. Aryans are the founders, Asians the guardians, and we, Ludmila, Mr. L., and I, the ravagers. Albert Einstein is a demon. Sigmund Freud gnaws at civilization like a rat. Hitler is an angel.

"Would you like to take a walk to the insane asylum?" Ludmila asked.

Then I said, "You shouldn't underestimate the origins of people—to whom and when they are born—if you hope for the world to be more beautiful tomorrow than it was yesterday."

Ludmila knew she was beautiful. There were days when people would stop on the street and just stare at her; even I told her quite frequently that her mother and father had turned out a real prize. But to her at times it seemed that her black eyes might be a minus rather than a plus, particularly in combination with her light-blond hair, which, for safety's sake, she began to cut short in the style of the mikado.

"If there were no girls like you running around in the world," I had said to her, "it wouldn't be so easy for them to think of themselves as so terribly purebred, right?"

December 16. Five times. Caraway seeds, salt. A kilo of bread flour. One hundred grams of margarine. Twelve marks. Two hundred grams of powdered sugar.

Once. A velvet muff with hamster fur on the inside.

Once. A bouillon cube.

December 17, 1943. I changed the candle, though frankly I don't know where I'll get another one after I use up these last two. I thought of speaking to the

Cabalist. Some people haven't left yet, while others went long ago. It was not because they knew prominent people, the way I knew Mr. L., but because they had a touch more or less of luck at any given moment, and in the final analysis, it's mostly luck that enables people to survive. Only once in a while a part of it is the opposite of luck, and I don't mean merely bad luck. I wonder where it is that my little rabbi is suing God. Is it just his thirst for revenge or the desire for justice? To condemn the one who himself condemns?

According to the Cabalist, the number four is good in the new calendar. When I wanted to know why, he smiled the way he would have at someone who hadn't gone to school, saying, "Four elements of life. One symbolizes a powerful and simple number or the sun. It also symbolizes a purpose. The start of new things. Nine symbolizes perfection, triunity, triplicity. Three is a number that writers believe in. It symbolizes the middle."

"Does it also stand for justice?"

"Don't you want a bit too much from one number?"

"Which number stands for love?"

"I can tell you that one stands for perseverance," he answered.

"What do I need numbers for if I can't find what I need in them?" I said. "I rather like what you said about old jugs with nothing in them, even though what you say about numbers you could really apply to anything."

He took me to the Delousing Station and gave me ten candles. On the way there, he told me about a man who had boasted about the kinds of things he had been able to survive, up until the last transport.

"A four following another four ensures heroic deeds.

It stands for stability within instability. Four winds, four corners of the earth, the four seasons of the year," said the Cabalist.

"I would prefer it if that four in the new calendar were to symbolize a house where you could live without fearing that you might be shipped off like cattle," I said.

"That depends on the kind of stuff people are made of," said the Cabalist. "Your friend Ludmila, the night before she went away, or so I'm told, was the subject of a contest between Harychek Geduld and another guy who came up with a way for one or the other or both, in that order, to woo her. The rest you know, don't you?" They bared their arms to the elbow. Then they clasped their arms upward so that the clasped elbow would hold a cigarette butt.

Lida and I saw them both do it. We saw the cigarette burn out, giving them blisters on their skin. And it was useless for Lida to tell them that it was nonsense mutilating themselves in that way before going away, and they told her that she didn't understand, until she found out that it was on her account.

"People do all kinds of things with their bodies when they know they're going east," I said. And I recalled that last night, what we did, how we sang, and played the guitar, and how happy Ludmila was.

"Thanks for the candles," I told him.

With Geduld went boys from German families that had been so German that the children belonged to the Hitlerjugend and their dads were in the army, until they got shoved in here because it turned out that they, like Milena, had a Jewish grandmother or two. Who knows who was settling what accounts with them. The Cabalist is easy to discuss it with, but I didn't want to keep him. He recited a slogan in German: *"Sorge nicht."* Don't worry. Or something to that effect. Numerologically speaking, it is number 10. "S" at the beginning is a one, "t" at the end is a zero.

Ludmila asked, "Is it true that your father was a dental technician?" By then we had been here alone for a long time, without our parents, like almost all the girls in L 410.

"He made his living that way," I replied. "I mean before. Here he made his living by stuffing horsehair into saddles in the German riding hall. The French ministers of commerce and the navy are there, along with two German generals—I mean former generals."

"He was in illustrious company," said Ludmila.

"Is that all you meant by that?"

Instead of a reply she asked, "Do you think he is still doing it?"

"Why do you ask when you know that there's no way I could know? It's at least six hundred miles from here. I haven't received any news whatsoever from them. He wasn't doing it anymore even when he was here."

"I heard from the Polish children who were brought in and then immediately sent away through the local Delousing Station, along with some medical personnel, about what they do with the gold teeth before they get rid of them. I mean the way they send them into the showers."

"How should I know, when at best my father is still there?"

"Because according to the children I saw, they do it to some people before rather than after they bathe them," said Ludmila.

I didn't respond. She was glaring at me as if she had to suffer because my father became a dentist. Or could she think that he had become the director of a spa? I don't know. She said, "I have the feeling that everything that's happening to me has somehow gone against time. As if I knew that I had to leave, but that I waited for my train to actually start moving before making it to the platform with boxes and a suitcase, if you know what I mean."

"Do you usually ride the express or the local?"

"The important thing is not what I ride but all the things that I'll miss," she answered. "What's important is that I always miss the main thing, whether I arrive on time or three days after something has happened, always at the wrong address, the wrong people, for the wrong reason."

It occurred to me much later that Ludmila might have thought at that time that I would survive it and there was no justice in the world, neither in the reaches we have no influence over nor in those belonging to us. We seem to have several faces and various faces for various occasions and for different people, different nights, and different moments.

Twice. Rubber bands for bell jars. Five marks. A medallion with a drawing of a beautiful, black-haired woman by Leonardo da Vinci.

It occurred to me that there might be two histories flowing next to each other, just like when old man O. said that every person lives an additional, secret life alongside his external one: the history of kings or countries or events, as well as the private history of people that includes not only what happened to them but that affects the fate of others. This is the unnoticed history. The forgotten history of ordinary people like old man O.,

Mr. L., Rabbi B., Ludmila, or Harychek Geduld. A
history of girls like Milena repeated over and over a
thousand times. I wondered, where is this likely to flow
out? Those unknown rivers of unknown people's lives,
gushing into an unknown sea.

I met Ernie H. in front of the Hamburg Barracks.
Skin and bones, wearing an elegant leather coat reaching almost to below his knees, and a shirt and tie, the
shirt collar one size too large. He was carrying a margarine box tied up with rope, containing all his belongings.
He said that he'd never been to Poland and that he'd
always had a great desire to visit foreign lands. And he
winked at me, as if he were on a journey to join the
Foreign Legion, merely going by way of Poland.

"I like to take the roundabout route," he said in his
thin voice.

"I'll join you soon and find out what it looks like,"
I said.

"Don't rush, give me some time, so I can get a better
supper for you," said Ernie. "Or rather breakfast, so
that I don't overextend myself at the start."

"Can I count on getting some elegant lady's bag?"

"Would you like a hatbox as well?" he asked.

They were calling out the last hundred, out of two
thousand. He waved his free hand at me. He trotted out
through the gate onto the ramp and over a board into a
car. In the railroad car he turned around, blowing me a
kiss. It seemed to me that this boy knew how to find fun
even as he landed in the greatest of quagmires.

I am alone, as I have seldom been before. My roommate is the only one I could possibly write a letter to.
"Dear rat, how have you been? First, my kind memories

and many greetings to you. I think of you incessantly—
what you are doing and what your prospects are for the
future. As far as I'm concerned, I try not to think about
anything. Dear rat, what shall we do when I use up all
my candles? Take care in the meantime; best regards.
Yours, Perla."

Before Ludmila and I reached the platform behind the
Hamburg Barracks, where the railroad cars were waiting
and the locomotive was about to be coupled, she said all
of a sudden, "Do you know what upsets me more than
almost anything else? I have never in my life received
a telegram."

"A telegram?" I repeated, astonished.

"Didn't it ever occur to you that there are things that
people all over the world take for granted, as much as
having a cup of tea with a roll when they wake up in the
morning?"

"As far as I know, telegrams are only sent when some
disaster happens, like when someone dies or something
like that. My father got a telegram when my grandmother, whom I don't remember too well, was taken to
the hospital."

"But people also receive telegrams saying that their
wife just had a baby, their friend got married, or they
get best wishes on their seventeenth birthday, or they've
won a hundred thousand," said Lidushka.

It was just like when she told me that she felt she had
been stripped of all her clothes and all her possessions
a long time ago. It had all taken place somewhere else
before it happened to her: the first day, when she was
given the star to sew on over her heart and when she
separated herself from the others and the others from

her. Then, when she had to hand over everything but fifty kilograms and was brought here, right up to now, to her standing at the station again, about to set out on a journey to somewhere, a place from which perhaps no one will return. And just as the people in Prague were glad in the end not to see them, because it wasn't pleasant to watch what had happened to them, so they themselves will be glad in the end when the Germans finish them off once and for all. She had had the same feeling when the Germans first came to Prague. As though everything had been stripped from her body; stripped stark naked, as if she had nothing but herself, and even that seemed suddenly to be too much. It was like an avalanche. One of those moods that come over people without their being able or knowing how to explain it. An imperceptible, inaudible avalanche, as if some unknown, strong arms were holding and squeezing all the life out of her. As though she were getting ready to be killed or be cut up or to cut herself up. We have all learned to wait for this to pass, but Ludmila turned it into a question: Why had she never in her life received or sent a telegram? She went in a dark suit and black wool stockings that I gave her, and her winter coat. She was slender and pale.

Once. A bottle of kerosene. A bag of coal. A hundred and fifty marks. A first-aid kit.

I began to write on the lady's stationery, having numbered the pages from one to a hundred. I felt like a widow. Is it true that people in the east are afraid not just of being killed but of being buried alive?

Rabbi B. has hanged himself. Somehow he found out that a German doctor had sent his children in the east to Camp D, barracks twenty-four, where he wanted to change the color of their eyes from brown to blue and of their hair from dark to fair, using injections containing poison and lead.

I dreamed again that the whole family was together; it was winter, and we went to the mountains. Papa rented a room in a stone house, with a large dining room, where we ate with some other people, all together. Everyone who wanted to eat had to hand in a card with his name and number on it, before being served by the headwaiter.

Once, I didn't get anything. The headwaiter told me with a smirk that he was sorry, but without my card I wouldn't get any dinner. I didn't know what to do; I was afraid that without dinner I might die of hunger before morning. I was weak and anemic, I was going downhill fast, this wasn't going to end well. Then I took a card belonging to a boy who had left it next to his plate. Suddenly we realized that this was our last supper. Everyone began to hurry up. Then the headwaiter said that whoever had no card was to go down into the valley immediately. It was crackling cold out. Although nobody said a word, we all knew that nothing good was waiting for those who went down into the valley. It was no longer a choice between good or bad, right or wrong, just or unjust, but between surviving or not surviving.

I didn't have much time to decide what to do. I wanted to return the card to the boy, but then I would have had to go down into the valley. But I must have known that if the boy were to die, he would die on account of and instead of me. I tried to delay it. But time kept rushing on. And at the same time, I felt as if I were much too young to die. I am seventeen. I began to scream.

* * *

I can't sleep and it seems to me that words keep running away or hiding from me. There's a lot of tension inside of me, containing my kind of fire, which I feel could burn up the whole world, with me in it, if someone asked me to. Once, Mr. L told me that instead of me he was sending the incurably ill on the transport. Later he stopped saying that.

Lida and I often talked about people who had escaped in the nick of time and were now somewhere on the ocean's most distant shore. Somebody counted up the billions it had cost. Lida had spoken with Harychek Geduld about it before the morning when she said that she had been born nine times, with Harychek Geduld correcting her that perhaps she had died nine times. I also remember how Laszlo Berkovich went away with his four small children, each of them having a straw bag that their father had woven for them, a basket, and a box. It's all mixed up with a gypsy or a Jewish song that he probably never even sang or played for me. He thought that he would never go, because he mended the German officers' wives' dishes, and wove baskets for them, and brooms and fish nets and net swings, something he had promised to but never did actually make for me. He was the only man who had ever asked me whether I was able to have children.

December 21. I had known for several days by then that the Luftwaffe officer would come by as long as he was still stationed here. I just didn't know when, and I don't know whether I actually wanted him to come or whether it was a test of something else for me. I stared at him standing in the doorway in his beautiful blue cloth coat, with a short sword low on his hip. He kept his hands in his pockets. He was smiling at me just as he had when he'd come for the second time; he noticed my surprise at seeing him, since I hadn't expected him to come just then. But then I found out what he was most interested in, the only thing he really wanted from me and, as he himself once admitted, the thing he was obsessed with as if nothing else existed. I was staring at him, at his beautifully cut coat with its wide lapels and two rows of silver buttons, most probably the good work of one of the local tailors, who sewed the uniforms of almost all the officers, as I knew from Mr. L. "Here I am again," he said. I looked at him.

"You look just like the last time, almost too good for the circumstances," he said. He looked around the room for some time, lifted the skylight with his elbow, let it drop again, and inspected the door as if it reminded him of something. Since I had bruises and had put some iodine from the first-aid kit on them, the odor of iodine was still hovering and I could see that he noticed it. He smiled as if it told him something. But he didn't ask me anything about it. He saw the straw mattress, how much wear and tear it had had in his absence. He saw the beams from which I had removed the picture of Franz Kafka given to me by Harychek Geduld long ago, and a dreamy postcard that I had glued on top of my diary to protect it from the humidity. He saw a candle on my Italian table with bricks stacked up in place of the missing fourth leg.

"It's never as bad in here as it seems from the outside," said the Luftwaffe officer.

"You've got a beautiful dagger," I said.

"You've got more things here than someone in your circumstances has any need for, Perla Sara," he said.

"I try to sell whatever I can, and what cannot be sold, I give away," I said.

"In Germany, women of your kind give and take, but don't give away," he said, smiling.

"I've never complained. I wouldn't have the courage to do it."

"We must not exaggerate," he went on. "The last time I was here, a golden light was streaming in through the skylight, and before I left, a rat was sitting on the stairs, thinking that it couldn't be seen in the dark."

"I hate to talk about rats, but I think about them quite often," I said. "It's cold in here. May I close the door?"

"You're dressed so lightly," he said.

"Isn't it cold in here?" I asked him.

"It's just like in the Casino," he answered in jest.

In my mind's eye I saw myself in an orange dress, cut like a ballet costume that my mother had bought me when I was five years old. I remember how my sister, who was three years older than I was, declared that if I wore it out into the street, people would think I was crazy. Nobody wore such dresses anymore, she told me. I have often remembered that dress here, thinking about what a fine appearance I would make at the German Casino. I hadn't heard any music for a long time, and I realized that in this cold weather, the Casino was surely closed.

The evening was just beginning. I lit the candle. It spread a flickering light around the garret as if it were jumping from wall to wall, from the floor to the ceiling, playing with the shadow of the officer and with my shadow.

"I almost didn't expect to find you here," he said.

"I'm still here," I replied.

"Are you hungry?"

He was still standing with his hands in his pockets, but I had enough experience with the kinds of things people carried in their pockets to realize now that he had come empty-handed.

"You can eat your fill," said the officer without offering me anything, and I could guess right away what he had in mind.

I only now noticed the remnants of food on his coat, wine stains, and grease stains. I tried to guess where he had come from. But he didn't appear drunk. On the contrary, he seemed to be on guard or at least carefree in a studied way, controlling his nonchalance from the first moment he walked in.

He looked well built and handsome, even though he was shivering from the cold until his face regained its regular color; for although it's cold in my room, you can't feel the December wind here. The blue color of his coat reminded me of three things all at once. Of the sky, the reason why pilots all over the world choose that color for their uniforms; of night; and of a third thing as well —his eyes were blue, just like mine, but lighter. And under his belt, strapped on by knitted silver braids made out of the same fabric as his epaulettes, he wore his dagger, a German sword.

"And you can warm yourself up and warm me up in the process," the officer said again.

And slowly he began to unbutton his coat, without asking me to help him. Then he took out of the side pocket of his coat, to my surprise, a flat-sided flask of French cognac.

"I'm glad I've found you here," he said.

"I too am glad you've found me here," I answered.

"Nothing is certain," he added.

He took a look around the garret, his eyes locating two cups on the shelf under the beam, which Harychek Geduld had given me last summer when he thought he was about to depart but didn't, and felt awkward asking for them back.

"People from all the blocks south of yours are going on a transport tomorrow that no one knows about yet," he said slowly. And he poured as much into both cups as he could, making them even.

"I've waited every day for the summons and I'm ready," I said. "I can get ready in less than five minutes."

"We all get what's ours in the end," said the officer.

Then he instructed me on how to drink, for I told him that I had never tasted French cognac before. He sat across from me, where he had sat once before and where Mr. L. used to sit.

"Do you like it?" he asked.

Instead of a reply, I told him that I had dreamed about him a few times. I described the dreams. I could see that he was pleased with what I had dreamed about him, even though I didn't tell him everything. I must have appeared compliant, as if he could step all over me if he wanted to.

"I hope I didn't ruin my reputation," said the officer. He began to unbutton his clothing. "So little and so beautiful," he said looking to me.

He found it particularly funny that demons are like people. I touched the cognac with the tip of my tongue.

"I knew you would come," I said. "It was like an eclipse, the closing of one's eyes, even though the sun shines or the candle is lit. And I wished that it would happen, before I left or before the end of the year."

"It's as I say, nothing is sure and you should be the first one to know that," he said.

In a short while he placed his coat under himself with its silk lining turned up, and lay in front of me without even asking that I take everything off. He placed his belt with the dagger on the side of the mattress opposite from where he had first sat down, so as to keep it handy or at least in sight. In his eyes there was something that hadn't been there before, neither the last time nor when he had been here for the first time. It was mist, as though he could see many things at once, though none too distinctly. It crossed my mind that it was some German dream of his that kept bringing him to me. Then he noticed something hurting him, and he pulled out a Parabela revolver from his breast pocket, placing it alongside his dagger.

I watched him take a sip, and then, sizing up the pistol and the sword, I said, "It isn't a real sword and it isn't a regular knife," and I was thinking of the knife given to me on the twelfth of November. And then I thought that the officer was staring the way Melissa once used to stare. He wanted me to drink, even though he said that the more slowly one drinks such cognac, the sweeter was the drowning of such sorrows as hunger, cold, and cheerlessness. And he began to speak of two things without explicitly saying them as he lay on the mattress, on top of his warm coat, quite handsome in body and in face: of everything he had seen and of how there was always a duality, as if to confirm his impression that guilt and innocence blur unrecognizably. At the same time, he mentioned that he wouldn't want me to see even a fraction of what he himself had experienced.

I didn't know whether he wanted me to pity myself or him as I listened to the details he chose to describe in order to convince me of those two things.

He brought up the case of the violinist who had played in the local café with his partner, a pianist and accordionist, and what happened to him in the east. How a colleague of the Luftwaffe officer, an army doctor, had sent his four children and his wife to the wrong side, while the violinist was playing. After his departure from here, the man had become a member of the baths band, which plays for people in front of the showers or on the ramp, his face showing a trace of gratitude for his own survival.

I didn't know what the wrong side was, though I could guess. And he brought up something Ludmila too had once mentioned: the mothers who had had to watch, while getting off the train, how the soldiers smashed the heads of their infants against a wall, and yet how it was possible to discern in the mothers' horror a thread by which they clung to life.

"Why does everyone want to live at almost any cost?" the officer wondered. He said that he himself offered women the choice of sending their children into the bathhouses as the condition for their going to work in the munitions factory, and how many mothers had given up their children, as if there were still a chance for them to make new ones.

And there was something else, just as astounding as the hundreds of thousands of people going to their own slaughter in utter resignation, so bewildering that he couldn't make any sense out of the fact that these were two sides of the same coin.

"I would go too if I were in their place," I said. "Why not? What is there to wait for?"

I tried to listen to the scratching of the rat under the floor, but the rat suddenly lapsed into silence.

"They tell us we'll find peace when they send us to settle the eastern territories."

The Luftwaffe officer smiled distractedly. "Do you like fire? I heard that all your people love fire. And that ashes represent so many things that a normal person cannot even remember them all."

"What things?" I asked.

"Pity or atonement," said the Luftwaffe officer, smiling. "Renunciation of sin. Purification and rebirth. Before they knew how to make soap out of bones, they probably used ashes for the same purpose. Have you ever heard of Ash Wednesday?"

"In school," I answered. "I had some Catholic girl friends."

"Fire and water are like brother and sister. You can wash up with water or choke on it."

"That's not how I look at it," I said.

"There's a lot of fire there, and not just in the ovens. There are holes eight meters long and deep like ovens, where the dead are fried like in a kitchen or in hell, whichever you like. As far as I can see, you have no idea at all about hell."

"I'm not that innocent," I answered.

"Be glad," the officer said, lost in thought. "Some people believe that your soul is in your shadow. Would you believe that it can be in your ashes? In the fire?"

"My soul lives in my memories." I smiled. "In what will be."

The Luftwaffe officer spoke, gaping blankly as when a woman strips in front of a blind man or when someone is talking to the deaf and dumb who can't even tell that they are being spoken to. Or a man having an affair with me who is deprived of such feelings as trust, conscience, or shame. And so I could ask myself whether it was still

flattering for me to know ahead of five thousand others
what to prepare for before morning arrives.

He was looking at me as a pilot looks down on a
destroyed city below, already without voice and shape,
burnt beyond recognition like pieces of a once-living
body—as if I too was without a soul anymore, as if I was
only a haze of what I had been before and could return
to reality only through his presence. Why didn't he go
into the German prison to choose his women?

Yet at the same time I was glad he was here, waiting
up for me for so long. His eyes were telling me of the
bombed cities and of their special scent—of the ashes,
the remnants of smoke. I thought about those cities and
I suddenly wondered why the Germans could not understand why it is that when others apply the same mea-
sures, they are only getting back what they have done
to those others.

I wondered whether I could ask him what I'd wanted
to ask a long time ago: What makes him so happy when
he kills? I expected he'd give me an answer that all men
who have ever killed rely upon: It was like hunger,
drought, or cholera—it had always existed. To kill or to
be killed. It was like being fond of animals, children,
nature. Or maybe he'd tell me that our people had never
been well off, even when they thought they were, or had
tried to gain advantage from evil governments, or gifts
of nature, or natural disasters. I was ready to tell him
he didn't have to repeat any of this for me, that I had
heard it many times before.

Finally, I asked him.

Instead of answering, he replied, "Have you ever
flown across the Channel and fallen into the ice-cold
sea?" He waited for me to answer, then continued,
"When they fish out our flyers because a favorable

stream has not carried them over as far as England, they're as frozen as pieces of an ice floe. A man's temperature cannot drop by more than five degrees, the same way it mustn't rise by that amount, or he won't survive. I could tell you how my doctor friends try to bring them back to life."

He looked at the disappearing December sun through the skylight in the roof. He looked at the white clouds, becoming first red then dark. Two ravens flew croaking overhead. The day was at its end. I started my last night in Theresienstadt. The candlelight became more telling.

"We don't know where the time lies for the frozen pilots who fall into the sea," the officer added. "The problem is not just resisting the saltwater."

He looked my body over, with a look that was familiar save for one new shade.

"The strongest, healthiest men and women of your age are being trained in comfortable bathtubs with ice-cold water. Then we warm them up. So far, animal heat has proved to be the most effective. The men cool down to the maximum, and then girls like you lie next to them. But some men refuse to be warmed and let others take their places in the bathtub."

I said, "I'm the first to say I don't like winter. I don't even have the right blankets."

I almost wished I could warm up some of our men with my body heat. Was he indicating something to me?

I too looked outside through the skylight. A December day that had chilled me since morning seemed suddenly mild. It occurred to me that the officer had blue eyes, like the cold sun, which don't warm me. Yet they were still like a sun in that they now really saw me, and not just my haze. Was he offering me the chance to train in the apparatus where the men freeze and then come

back to life with animal heat? Is this what was expected
of me? But then, it's not up to me to ask.

"It's ridiculous to expect that killing is only a bullet
in the forehead, a knife in the heart, or a rope around
the neck," the officer said, smiling, "even if you don't
know about this yet."

He was probably glad that I had begun to talk about
killing, but already I was unhappy that I had. "Every
child knows that," I said, "even if it doesn't yet know
whether it's Monday or Tuesday or how the date is
written on letters."

I didn't want to make a face as if I were in the ice-cold
water for a minute or a day, a night or a week. I didn't
want to look like a German flyer, shot down because he'd
been forcing his way where he had no business. I didn't
want to look like a prisoner in a comfortable enameled
bathtub, being tested to see what the human organism
can withstand from the outside and from within. Instead
of salt water, they pour chemicals from a bottle into the
bathtub. I didn't want to look like a girl pressing against
someone who'd already frozen in order to breathe life
back into him. How can one think for so long that his
life has a higher value than my life, or Lida's life, or Mr.
L.'s, Papa's, Mama's . . . ? But in the eyes of the
Luftwaffe officer, a lie was like sincerity with which he
was decorating me.

It occurred to me what made the officer a liar even
though he was telling me the truth—even though he's
a much better liar than Mr. L. or Harychek Geduld or
Ernie H. Better than people who always lied to me in
order to get what they would have gotten even without
lying.

Mr. L. told me that when one looks at a tree long
enough, he'll discover what makes this tree different
from all of the others, unique, unrepeatable. So I sud-

denly knew why the officer lies, even though he is telling the irrevocable truth about the shot-down Luftwaffe pilots and the enameled bathtubs filled with ice-cold water. Was he waiting to know whether I would see in him that single tree despite all the other trees?

I had a feeling like the one I had with Ludmila the last time, when we went for a walk along the Wallstrasse in the Block E VII by the mental hospital, after the loonies had left for the east. The Council of Elders had established a home for the aged, but nothing had been done about it yet. I was looking at the officer's handsome face, at his neck and the place where he did not shave anymore, where the beard stopped growing.

The wind was squealing outside, and it came blowing in through the skylight. Somewhere on the roof, it broke a shingle in two. The shingle fell down onto the cobblestone pavement with a crash and shattered. The officer paused. He must have been sure that I was hanging on his every word.

Where is the limit beyond which guilt is no longer measured, as it was measured by my father, the little rabbi, or Mr. L.? I thought that the Luftwaffe officer lied in order to make his words ring more true than the truth. But still I was flattered all the time that he was here with me. A lie for him will do as much as a revolver, an airplane machine gun, or the ice-cold water in the English sea or a comfortable bathtub. But I didn't feel like forgiving the fact that he considered a lie to be a virtue for which one receives a deserved decoration.

Where was Mr. L. to explain it to me? Or the rabbi? The Luftwaffe officer's eyes asked me if I understood. He had magnanimity in his eyes, which wiped out the difference between him and the enemy or me for at least a little while.

At the same time a flash of sadness ran across his face,

an expression indicative of people who are dependent on themselves alone. And there was another side to his languor: his enthusiasm for himself, his admiration of himself. He looked at me as at a dog, as if he were looking into a mirror.

"Everyone gets what he deserves in the end," he said at last.

"I would like to know sometimes what goes on in other people's heads," I answered.

He looked at me as if he were looking where my yesterdays had disappeared to, because as far as tomorrow was concerned, he knew as well as I where my journey would take me. For a while he rested as if he too were lying in a white enameled bathtub without the ice-cold water he was scared of in the English sea. He interpreted my smile in his own way. That dark, which I don't understand to this day, connected us, as if the reflection of all the thoughts about death and killing was a bodily appetite, some hidden impulse, a struggle to prove with this animal heat something in one's self. Something that animals have, that people once had, according to Mr. L., but that got lost from us and returns only as an echo. I almost started feeling sorry that I'd lost it. I smiled at him the way I had once smiled at Mr. L.

I drank my cognac so slowly that the Luftwaffe officer poured a bit from my cup into his. We went on talking for a while longer, and I could see that he was gazing at his own body and at my mouth, as if seeing nothing but my lips and in the end not wanting anything else.

His body was awakening with every passing instant as he observed my lips. Maybe he was saying something to himself, whispering, but I don't think I heard it or else I couldn't understand it. I knew what he wanted, and it wasn't the first time he would get it from me.

On his face and in the expression of his eyes, which he had partly closed like a cat, I could observe each of my touches. There were moments when his expression grew distant, as if he were no longer here, as if he were looking inside himself or touching something as far away as death or the mystery connected with the birth of man.

Then I observed his hands, as he stretched out his fingers, as if wanting to touch something intangible, grasping it and then clenching his fist, opening up his hand again and pressing it to his eyes, no longer wanting to see anything.

I could hear the rat rattling in the corner under the floorboard.

The whole time I was helped by the knowledge that I would leave on a transport in the morning. They leave inexorably, only empty cars returning, pulled by different or the same locomotives and with different engineers aboard—Czech, German, or Dutch, depending on the station or the depot that has engines available for yet another transport, a thousand, two thousand, three thousand, and in the last few weeks, always five thousand people all at once. It felt something like when a river gets ready to absorb a drop of dew or the other way around, when a drop gets ready for the river. For a long time, I saw it as some raindrops or dirt from a puddle or as a drop of blood just like when I scraped myself before and tried to stop the bleeding with iodine, or like the spittle of some man or animal. And it was just as helpful to know that in all likelihood no one would ever find out and that the silence that had made Mr. L. and then little Rabbi B. so nervous wouldn't be ruffled, not even so much as when a stone plops into a lake, its surface rippled and then the ripples vanishing as if they

hadn't ever been there. I didn't need to think of remorse
or embarrassment, for if I did, it would just fade away
anyway, with every turn of the wheels of the train, and
the train moving ever farther along the route that it had
traveled so often already, there and back and there
again, countless times, during the day or at night, in the
spring, in the summer, in the fall, or in the winter,
through any weather.

I thought of the women who believed that they would
become purer if they smeared themselves with what
children are born of, or of the girls who believed that
they would become healthier, stronger, and more attractive if they swallowed a great many seedlings all at once,
and of Ludmila, my mother, Milena, and all the girls I
have known. I could imagine our morning train, moving
along day and night, two days and two nights, through
Ustí nad Labem, Dresden, and Katowitz, just as Mr. L.
had once described it, the traces of everything that had
ever happened anywhere outside the train growing more
distant.

The Luftwaffe officer was clean, exuding the aroma of
tobacco, of other women's perfumes, and of food. I heard
the sighs of his body and the sighs coming out of his
mouth. He kept his eyes closed, and I knew he wasn't
thinking of anything, unlike myself, who had to think
incessantly of the rat in the corner, for it made a lot of
noise.

I didn't feel like letting myself go to the point of
envying the rat for staying behind so long as no one traps
her or poisons her and then throws her into the river or
into a fire. Though at one particular instant I was quite
close to the rat, comparing my possibilities with hers.

"You little Jewish whore, you," said the German
officer. "Perla S."

I was also thinking about the skin of the German

women I have known here, who would be in the places for which I would set out tomorrow morning. Was it true, as rumor had it, that some of them bathed in blood? Or that they make their lamp shades out of the skin of virgins or of young men who have no wrinkles?

When the Luftwaffe officer was here the last time, he brought some Vaseline in the pocket of his winter coat because his lips were chapped from the eastern cold and wind, and he wanted me to smear my lips as well.

He couldn't understand how I could hold out so long and look the way I looked. Then I was thinking of how happy some mothers were while still anticipating the birth of their children, embracing their husbands and whispering what people whisper at such moments, as if it were the irrevocable truth—and then they saw, to the extent they could stand to watch, the remnants of their infants thrown against the walls. Some parents perished fairly early on, before their children had the chance to blame them for their own fate. Though it was also the same the other way around.

Just for an instant I was again a captain, as in my dream, and the captain was in my shoes. And for a fraction of a second there were demons who looked like some of us. My mouth expanded almost simultaneously with the sigh that tore out of the Luftwaffe officer's throat, as if it weren't his voice but a voice no less distant than the stars. From underneath the floor the old rat began making noise again.

At the beginning, while we still had the chance to talk and I asked the officer about what method was used to sterilize women in the east, he answered that it probably didn't pertain to my mother anymore; but when I mentioned Milena or Ludmila, he said that X rays were beamed between their legs, unless a surgical procedure was involved.

"What would you want to tell your children?" he asked.

But from every word he said I could hear how funny it was for him to think that I might have children someday, wanting to tell them something I would apparently never tell them.

My thoughts began to unwind in the one direction from which they had until then been charging. It was like a dynamo, expanding the strength it had just acquired. I will not speak about my teeth, the way Ludmila had done occasionally. Nor about the beautiful sword that lay so close to me, along with the pistol. And just as close to me, on the pile with my writing supplies, there lay the letter opener that I had received along with a pencil and a bar of soap; I remembered being given it as distinctly as if it had just happened. It all became one blur, as if everything were coming together within me to create a single moment.

And I don't feel like speaking about the spot to the side of the throat that is even more sensitive than the groin. Nor about the scream, when I pressed my teeth as forcibly as I could, like a rat wanting to extricate itself from a trap, or about the scream accompanied by sweeping arm motions. There weren't many of these, as I recall it now, but they all became tangled up in a single knot that I don't want to unravel.

Then it seemed to me that I noticed that in her nest underneath the floor in the corner of the attic, the rat became quiet. I could hear nothing for a long while, not even a single scratch. I waited to hear it again.

Mrs. Itsikson, who had worked in a bar before the war, told me what she had been told when she reported to her new job at the age of seventeen: "You can be glad that you were born a woman. I'm not saying that you'll never have to starve, that your wardrobe will always be full of clothes, or that you'll get a countless number of invitations to go on trips. But you will be far better off with regard to all these things than if you were not standing here now, waiting for the first male guests who will gladly pay for you if you are nice to them. Most often men will gladly do everything for you—at least for one evening, or day, or night."

Then she told me that it was up to each woman separately as to just what class she would reach. It was like that for the rest of her life.

Although I never met her again, what she told me has remained with me because it was the most important thing she could have said.

The German woman in the east whom we have gotten some news about was said to have taken baths in an enamel bathtub in her army barracks, her white skin reflected in the bathtub's contents like a wild strawberry sitting in a plate of whipped cream. They say she used to invite her military colleagues from the SS and SA into the bathroom, where she was sitting straight up, with her straw-colored hair combed upward, smiling as if she were savoring their admiration.

When I reread the last entry, it struck me that it might also be reversed. There are times when children are ashamed for having survived their parents. But this shame comes from the impossibility of sparing someone from things he ought to be spared from, but from which no one has been saved so far, whether he wanted to or didn't, tried to or not.

Some rumors have penetrated from the east that Freddy Hirsch poisoned himself after the Germans killed the children that he cared for. The German officer or the German doctor or the Polish Kapo must have sold him a gram of cyanide.

I have just heard that he once asked the SS Sturmbahnführer responsible for transport where they had last murdered and robbed. They found Freddy Hirsch beaten senseless. He was from Aachen, had studied medicine at Oxford before the war, and had learned Czech. He never buckled under the Nazis. They both hated and respected him. They could not beat the resistance out of him. They could only send him to the east.

Then I thought mostly about Ludmila and only after that about myself and still later about the Luftwaffe officer. I was thinking about something she thought was awful, even though it was innocent. Every woman, as Ludmila knew without ever experiencing it, was closer to it in such a moment than she thinks, if she intends to do what I ultimately did.

When she was nine, Lida was dancing alone in her room when her papa surprised her. She never forgave him for it, not even now when he was already in the east.

I got ready for the scream, which sounded just like when men sometimes shout.

I wasn't thinking of the rough force that both enters into and slips away from a man. I was not surprised that it was not an instant end, just instant pain, so violent that it swept away everything that remained of one's presence of mind, giving me time to grab the letter opener. I don't know anymore whether all the pressures inside me were released, as if I were feeling everything together in a new shape, all the crying and the shadows of the people who had been. I don't know, I really don't. Perhaps I only know that at times you can feel the firm ground under your feet as if it were hell. And then you feel what so many people have felt before, that we are really alone. Perhaps it's connected with something else that makes people alone, whatever the time. Only it bursts open sometimes, like a volcano erupting.

Is the decision to act made of the same stuff as defenselessness? Is man like moist soil that can be molded into various shapes, so the most repulsive becomes most beautiful, and the shapeless most firm?

Maybe yes and maybe no. But at the same time I know that there's no one I could tell about what happens when those who are screaming in their death throes have mutilated or killed off everyone who could have heard them and come to their aid.

I could talk to the rat, who will never give me any response but who keeps scratching on the wood, reminding me of her existence. Some rats can supposedly jump as high as the shoulders of an adult person, like cats.

We possess the most unexpected gifts. Flesh and bones, eyes, muscles, blood. Whatever a person thinks. It's not yet morning, though it's not too far off. I don't know why the Luftwaffe officer told me as much as he did, even about the final hours of the first secretary of the Council of Elders, whom Mr. L. had accompanied to the platform for his transport east. He was kept in a bunker for a year, wearing only the shirt he had arrived in and a single set of underwear.

The bunker was dark, only big enough for one person. He probably didn't need to mention that it could easily have turned the man into a hunk of meat, were it not for his willpower. He was the same man who had been so concerned about having the greatest possible number of young people survive in order to dig wells in a distant land, covered by desert and a deeply burrowed history.

He had probably not been forgiven by very many of the
older people. Who knows? After a year he was dragged
out of the bunker, allowed to wash and change his
clothes, and was invited to the office of the Commandant
of Camp D, where he was met by his wife, mother, and
son. Next to them the German officers looked as if they
had stepped from the pages of a fashion magazine, fresh
and clean-shaven. The Luftwaffe officer gave his account
in such detail that I had no reason to doubt that he had
seen it with his own eyes. The Commandant asked the
former secretary of the Council of Elders, in front of the
members of his family, whether he still held such a
strong vision of the Promised Land, the vision that had
caused him to reduce the rations of the old people when
he was given the opportunity to distribute provisions,
allotting food only to those who might one day help to
accomplish his dream.

Instead of replying, the man supposedly just smiled.
The Commandant's aide-de-camp took out a nine-milli-
meter parabel and shot his mother before the man's
eyes. The Commandant repeated his question. Then the
aide-de-camp shot the man's son and wife. Finally they
shot him.

At last I understood why the Luftwaffe officer had told
me all those things. From underneath the floor, the rat
could be heard very faintly. It seemed to me that the
sounds of the rat were the truth, that the words spoken
by the Luftwaffe officer were true, that life, even if it
consisted of nothing but lies, is the only true life.

While the officer was still standing in the doorway to
my attic in his warm, beautiful coat, with his hands in
his pockets, appraising me like an animal or like a
person who is far beneath the level of the one doing the
assessing, he asked me suddenly whether I still had

hope that things would change, I mean for me. And he asked what it was that might please me.

"Do you still get your bread ration?"

"Once in a while."

And then I said, "I'm still out of the mainstream of everything, like this old rat. I understand a great many things that she does."

And when the officer peered at me distrustfully: "When I can wash up, lie down, and watch the stars, that's all I need to be reminded that the world still turns on its axis."

"None of your people had, has, or will have the courage to see through to the bottom," the officer said curtly. And then he gave me another look, as if it made no sense to discuss such things with me. "It's like a water system on a river, one, two, three, maybe five miles long," he added. "Past each water gate, past each additional floodgate nearer to the sea, there is less water than before, till it becomes so shallow that you can see the pebbles at the bottom, dead fish, leeches, and everything that lies far underneath."

He watched me as if he were seeing a desert instead of the sea, fish and water lice instead of people, all the while standing on top of a big mountain. And he watched me close my eyes so as to avoid seeing that this was in fact the bottom.

"To some people, life offers everything," I said. I was trying to catch the sounds of the rat.

Ludmila asked me once, quite earnestly, how to arrange it so that she could see only those aspects of the truth that she could bear, just as when Mr. L. refused to even so much as talk about the old rat that was always here, even though at times he could hear no scratching. All this spilled over into the first scream, which almost frightened me even though I had expected it. With the second scream, somewhat weaker than the first, something else besides the pain could be heard, before being swallowed by blackout. Even far weaker hands than mine would have been capable of doing the rest.

"Maybe life does not offer all that much," I added.

It is late. It's still dark out. From a hole in the corner, as big as a man's fist, the rat's eyes stare out. They look up and then down. It's as simple as sewing on a button. The straw mattress is soaked and still more is being soaked up; the blue aviator cloth and the bluish silk lining have changed color. In a moment I'll untie the bottom pocket of the mattress and hide everything, as if I were stuffing it up with more straw and rags for which I'll have no further need, and then I'll turn it over. When I go away, the rat will stay alone here, in the dark, with nothing to fear.

A few hours remain. I know I can't take a single line of what I have written with me. The handbag that I was given is made of a black shiny waxed cloth and has a sturdy lock. I know of a place behind one of the beams where I used to keep my money and the diary, in case someone uninvited were to show up in my absence. It doesn't leak there and I'll just stick it in a bit deeper than I have done so far.

I have sold or given away most of my belongings. I'll travel with a rather elegant suitcase, but it will be virtually empty, in case we are met at the disinfection station by young men from the local Home for Wayward Children, and I won't cry if they take everything. I know that for some people, if our fate is any guide, next year is so far off that they won't get even to within several weeks of it.

Before I go, I'll rinse my mouth with ice water. I don't feel like writing anymore. It's possible that one can write only so long as it's in some small measure, at least, a game, a kind of race against time. Besides, one can't write from either joy or sadness alone.

I keep coming back to something Ludmila asked me: "When people die, the best of them want to leave something behind. But do you know what I want? I want to leave absolutely nothing. Do you believe me?"

"Why are you telling me this?" I asked. "I have to believe you, since you are saying it so convincingly."

"Even if there were something that could remain behind, I want it to bleed to the last drop, exactly the way I will," Ludmila said.

Her words sounded like an echo of something that already had been said or had happened, that had already had a name and had brought something familiar to mind.

"I understand it or at least I think I understand it," I said. "You simply want to kill, so long as you will be killed. It's as if you were thirsty, but instead of water you wanted to drink justice."

I had the feeling that this was so deep inside us that nobody would ever rip it out unless he were to kill us, but even then he wouldn't kill it with us.

"Between justice and revenge, there is a line so thin that I can no longer see it," said Lida. "Have you noticed that everything around you, people, things, time, the past, as well as the outlook for the future—even if it were to come between tomorrow and a thousand years hence—will teach you how to kill, even if you were born a lamb?"

*　*　*

I keep thinking about the stars that are long dead by now but that go on casting their light, yesterday, tomorrow, and for who knows how much longer. I'll work hard to put up a barricade here when I go away. But I'll leave the skylight open, so that snow and rain and then some dust and ashes can come in and so that my rat can be helped by other rats, and the rats by birds, worms, and insects. I don't want to look toward the straw mattress anymore. My voice tells me, as always, when there is truth in what I write. But I am no longer filled with excitement as I used to be each time I knew that what I wrote was the truth. I know that excitement may be deceptive now.

I am seventeen, but I feel as old as the trees, the wind, the rivers. As the stars, light, and darkness. My vulcan-fiber suitcase is two steps away from me, so that I'll be ready when the man from Central Registry in the Magdeburg Barracks, where Mr. L. officiated for so long, knocks on the door downstairs.

When I was four years old, I used to dance and sing for anyone who asked, in our house, on the street, almost anywhere. When I was twelve, I told myself that I should be a good girl, more unselfish every day. I took a secret oath about what I would strive to accomplish in my life. At thirteen, my body and my head made an agreement. At sixteen, I vowed to learn everything that a person like me could learn. And to strive to feel happy for everything worth feeling happy about.

Before the Luftwaffe officer came, I dreamed that I was singing and dancing the way I used to dance when I was four years old. The dance itself was different, and not only because a lot of water had flowed under the bridge, though the feeling of dancing was the same. But in spite of my dancing, I felt as if I were the last person in the world. In my dream I wanted to ask my mother why there had to be so much misery before man could change. Change for the better? For the worse? I don't know, I just don't know. Don't know.

Once, Ludmila and I talked about the stars. She thought that only what is distant is beautiful. To this I said maybe everything that is beautiful is good. "Earlier, maybe what was beautiful was good," said Ludmila. "Now only what does not exist is beautiful." She laughed.

I feel closer to the rat than to anything else. Rats don't worry about tomorrow. I can imagine the rat tomorrow, as far as that goes. Maybe I'll think about the rat more than about anything else, even on the train. I already feel that her teeth are my teeth, her eyes are my eyes, a piece of rat's heart lies in my chest.

Even at the end of the journey, when they chase us out of the railroad cars, the image of the rat will still be with me, what she munches on, and how she will outlive me. Everything will remain with the rat. I don't have to worry about her name, her date of birth, her address. Rats can do without names, without numbers, without return addresses.

Down at the ramp stands a freight train, cattle cars. It won't rain, snow, nor will the wind blow on us. Fifty cars. We will be packed in like sardines. Before they seal the doors, they will throw a sack of boiled potatoes at our heads, and shove into the hands of the nearest person a pail filled with water, which, after we've drunk it dry, can serve as lavatory.

It is cold, the sun is shining. Snow lies on the towers

that surround the Theresienstadt Fortress, white, without footprints. The stone squares and the bricks from which the night wind has blown the snow glisten like ice. The locomotive puffs away, and the engineer gazes at the mountains. The air is clean. A feeling of warmth breathes from the locomotive.

In a while I will climb down the wooden stairs and for the last time hear them squeak as if they led their own secret life, like everything and everybody else.

Inside me I can hear the echoes of voices that at times arrive as inaudibly as the light of those extinguished stars. If I had to, I would do it again. It is as if I am something like an antenna, connected to everything. I am wearing my best coat with a man's fox collar sewn onto it, and I am probably pale, just as Milena, Melissa F., and Mr. L. were as they left.

In a little while I will be in a railroad car, with the number 44 on my neck. I know from experience that the organization of the Reichsbahn is perfect. I don't need to worry that we might not leave. I feel empty, as if I have no marrow in my bones, as if my existence has been stripped naked while being covered by invisible darkness, and at the same time, I feel inside me the presence of people who have gone away, are going, and are still to go. People I know, as well as those unknown, are with me. I am about to go where almost everyone else has gone.

December 22, 1943

PERLA S.